ON YOUR MARKS

More anthologies available from
Macmillan Collector's Library

ON YOUR MARKS

Selected writings about all kinds of sports

Edited and introduced by
MARTIN POLLEY

MACMILLAN COLLECTOR'S LIBRARY

This collection first published 2022 by Macmillan Collector's Library
an imprint of Pan Macmillan
The Smithson, 6 Briset Street, London EC1M 5NR
EU representative: Macmillan Publishers Ireland Ltd, 1st Floor,
The Liffey Trust Centre, 117–126 Sheriff Street Upper,
Dublin 1, D01 YC43
Associated companies throughout the world
www.panmacmillan.com

ISBN 978-1-5290-7581-6

Selection, introduction and author biographies © Martin Polley 2022

The permissions acknowledgements on p. 223 constitute
an extension of this copyright page.

Casing design and endpaper pattern by Mel Four
Typeset by Jouve (UK), Milton Keynes
Printed and bound in China by Imago

Visit www.panmacmillan.com to read more
about all our books and to buy them.

Contents

Introduction

MARTIN POLLEY

I often set my new students a challenge when we start my course on sports history. We try to answer the question 'What is a sport?' We set up a range of characteristics that we think something should have for us to class it as a sport, like competitiveness, physicality, rules, and regulations, and then run many different activities through these models to see what sticks. The obvious activities like football, netball, swimming, and cricket always get universal approval, while extreme ironing, ballroom dancing, esports, and chess tend to provoke more debate. We all quickly see that so much depends on culture and history. What people from one time or place might class as a sport can just as easily appear to another age as not sporting at all. Today, we might baulk at ratting and bull-baiting, which our ancestors were very happy with as part of their sporting lives. Similarly, they would not know where to begin with the new Olympic sports of skateboarding and breakdancing. In class, we end up concluding that there is no easy answer to the question, as historical and cultural variations stand in the way of an answer that will suit everybody.

The collection of writings you have in your hand is a perfect illustration of this truth. By sampling a range of written sources from the past 400 years, we can quickly see that people knew a sport when they saw one, without anyone defining it for them. They knew about the kinds of excitement and exhilaration that a sport can bring to the player and the spectator, and how individuals can become a part of something so much bigger – teams, obviously, but communities too – through sport. But these writings also tell us about variety, and about how so many different activities have made sense as sports across the centuries.

But these aren't just any old sources on sport. This collection, which spans 350 years, draws together novelists, playwrights, poets, diarists, and travel writers who all spent some of their time and creative energy in writing about sport. There are contributions here from some of our finest literary figures: you'll find for example, William Shakespeare, George Orwell, Fanny Burney, Samuel Pepys, Winifred Holtby and Charles Dickens. This is a disparate group of writers, all of whom found something in the sports of their times that resonated with them.

Telling stories has always been part of sport. Sporting events, like stories, have a start, a middle, and an end. They have action and excitement, heroes and villains, drama and denouement, comedy and tragedy. Sometimes, they even have a moral. In the creative writing and reportage captured here, our authors see sport as a place where people express themselves with skill, creativity, and ingenuity, with unpredictable outcomes and results. Sport offers up many different devices for story-tellers. It can set the scene for their characters, and it can serve to advance the action. Authors can load sport with metaphors and symbols for their story's major themes, and they can use sport as a place in which characters can learn truths about themselves and others.

One of sport's biggest attractions is the excitement it can bring, and our authors knew it. For some, the excitement lies in the playing. Think of Hughes's Tom Brown, deep in the action in his first football match as a new boy at Rugby School, or the tension that mounts with each arrow fired in Scott's famous archery contest in *Ivanhoe*. At its best, sport can even allow the player to transcend their everyday life, a state captured best by the tragic Sorley in his ode to cross-country running, or by Forster's joyful wild swimmers. We also have many insights here on the excitement that watching can bring, whether it is the carnival atmosphere of Derby Day that captures Moore's Esther Walter, or the visceral engagement that the crowd feel with every blow landed by Hazlitt's boxers in the 'The Fight'.

Above the individual level, sport also plays a role in creating communities. Anyone who has ever supported a team at any level knows this: the players stand as our proxies as 'we' play against 'them'. Many of our authors have explored this relationship, and considered the dynamics at play when a team stands for 'a new community', as Priestley put it, 'all brothers together for an hour and a half'. This feature of sport also comes through in the descriptions of community sports festivals that Head and Burney describe, and, as Graves shows us with the sticky end that his puritanical preacher comes to, woe betide any outsider who tries to tell a group of people to stop their sports.

But it's not all fun and togetherness. There is a lot of brutality against animals here, with the extracts that deal with hunting, shooting, ratting, and cockfighting suggesting that sport has long been a realm in which people like to show off the ability to dominate nature. Authors such as Cobbett, Thackeray, and Pepys broadly approved of this state of affairs, even if they criticized some of the people involved: indeed, we can see the themes of excitement and community-building run through them.

The cockpit, the shoot, and the hunt were places to see and be seen, and places of social bonding.

And, of course, there is nostalgia and, in some texts, a great sadness at the passing of time and the loss of youth. Thompson's poem 'At Lord's' captures this mood with great pathos, as he refuses to watch a cricket match for fear that he will only see the ghosts of the players he watched in his youth. Holtby's disabled soldier angrily reflects on how losing a limb in the war has deprived him of sport, and Housman muses on how his 'athlete dying young' has saved himself the ignominy of growing old and losing his ability. I've included these extracts as these authors remind us, with heart-breaking realism, that sport is not just a place of fun and excitement: it's also a realm of failed dreams, lost youth, and missed opportunities.

I hope that you enjoy these meditations on sport by some of our great writers. Read them for the pleasure that they can bring in their own right, and use them as a starting point for thinking more deeply about sport and the meanings that we attach to it. It's never only a game.

ON YOUR MARKS

WILLIAM SHAKESPEARE
1564–1616

Playwright and poet William Shakespeare was born and raised in Stratford-upon-Avon and worked in London. His histories, comedies, and tragedies, as well as his sonnets and other poems, are amongst the most famous texts in the English language. He used sporting images and metaphors in many of his works. In his comedy *As You Like It*, written around 1599, Shakespeare used a wrestling match between Duke Frederick's court wrestler, Charles, and the lead character Orlando as a way to develop story-lines around love, honour, and family. The scene here also suggests the tough rural wrestling culture of the time, with the hardened Charles having already beaten, and possibly killed, three opponents before he even meets Orlando.

from *As You Like It*

LE BEAU Fair Princess, you have lost much good
    sport.

CELIA Sport? Of what colour?

LE BEAU What colour, madam? How shall I
    answer you?

ROSALIND As wit and fortune will.

TOUCHSTONE Or as the Destinies decrees.

CELIA Well said, that was laid on with a trowel.

TOUCHSTONE Nay, if I keep not my rank —

ROSALIND Thou losest thy old smell.

LE BEAU You amaze me, ladies. I would have told
    you of good wrestling, which you have lost the
    sight of.

ROSALIND Yet tell us the manner of the wrest-
    ling.

LE BEAU I will tell you the beginning; and, if it
    please your ladyships, you may see the end, for
    the best is yet to do, and here, where you are, they
    are coming to perform it.

CELIA Well, the beginning that is dead and buried.

LE BEAU There comes an old man and his three
    sons —

CELIA I could match this beginning with an old tale.

LE BEAU Three proper young men, of excellent
    growth and presence —

ROSALIND With bills on their necks: 'Be it known unto all men by these presents.'

LE BEAU The eldest of the three wrestled with Charles, the Duke's wrestler, which Charles in a moment threw him, and broke three of his ribs, that there is little hope of life in him. So he served the second, and so the third. Yonder they lie, the poor old man their father making such pitiful dole over them that all the beholders take his part with weeping.

ROSALIND Alas!

TOUCHSTONE But what is the sport, Monsieur, that the ladies have lost?

LE BEAU Why, this that I speak of.

TOUCHSTONE Thus men may grow wiser every day. It is the first time that ever I heard breaking of ribs was sport for ladies.

CELIA Or I, I promise thee.

ROSALIND But is there any else longs to see this broken music in his sides? Is there yet another dotes upon rib-breaking? Shall we see this wrestling, cousin?

LE BEAU You must if you stay here, for here is the place appointed for the wrestling, and they are ready to perform it.

CELIA Yonder, sure, they are coming. Let us now stay and see it.

Flourish. Enter Duke Frederick, Lords, Orlando,
  Charles, and attendants

DUKE Come on. Since the youth will not be
  entreated, his own peril on his forwardness.

ROSALIND Is yonder the man?

LE BEAU Even he, madam.

CELIA Alas, he is too young; yet he looks successfully.

DUKE How now, daughter and cousin? Are you
  crept hither to see the wrestling?

ROSALIND Ay, my liege, so please you give us
  leave.

DUKE You will take little delight in it, I can tell
  you, there is such odds in the man. In pity of the
  challenger's youth I would fain dissuade him, but
  he will not be entreated. Speak to him, ladies, see
  if you can move him.

CELIA Call him hither, good Monsieur Le Beau.

DUKE Do so: I'll not be by.

He stands aside

LE BEAU Monsieur the challenger, the Princess
  calls for you.

ORLANDO I attend them with all respect and
  duty.

ROSALIND Young man, have you challenged
  Charles the wrestler?

4

ORLANDO No, fair Princess. He is the general challenger; I come but in as others do, to try with him the strength of my youth.

CELIA Young gentleman, your spirits are too bold for your years. You have seen cruel proof of this man's strength; if you saw yourself with your eyes, or knew yourself with your judgement, the fear of your adventure would counsel you to a more equal enterprise. We pray you for your own sake to embrace your own safety, and give over this attempt.

ROSALIND Do, young sir, your reputation shall not therefore be misprized: we will make it our suit to the Duke that the wrestling might not go forward.

ORLANDO I beseech you, punish me not with your hard thoughts, wherein I confess me much guilty to deny so fair and excellent ladies anything. But let your fair eyes and gentle wishes go with me to my trial: wherein if I be foiled, there is but one shamed that was never gracious; if killed, but one dead that is willing to be so. I shall do my friends no wrong, for I have none to lament me; the world no injury, for in it I have nothing: only in the world I fill up a place which may be better supplied when I have made it empty.

ROSALIND The little strength that I have, I would it were with you.

CELIA And mine, to eke out hers.

ROSALIND Fare you well. Pray heaven, I be deceived in you!

CELIA Your heart's desires be with you!

CHARLES Come, where is this young gallant that is so desirous to lie with his mother earth?

ORLANDO Ready, sir, but his will hath in it a more modest working.

DUKE You shall try but one fall.

CHARLES No, I warrant your grace, you shall not entreat him to a second, that have so mightily persuaded him from a first.

ORLANDO You mean to mock me after; you should not have mocked me before. But come your ways!

ROSALIND Now Hercules be thy speed, young man!

CELIA I would I were invisible, to catch the strong fellow by the leg.

Orlando and Charles wrestle

ROSALIND O excellent young man!

CELIA If I had a thunderbolt in mine eye, I can tell who should down.

A shout as Charles is thrown

DUKE (*coming forward*) No more, no more.

ORLANDO Yes, I beseech your grace, I am not yet
    well breathed.

DUKE How dost thou, Charles?

LE BEAU He cannot speak, my lord.

DUKE Bear him away.

Attendants carry Charles off

SAMUEL PEPYS
1633–1703

Samuel Pepys was a Member of Parliament and administrator of the Royal Navy and is most famous for the million-word diary which he kept throughout the 1660s. As well as covering the decade's political life and famous events in London, such as the Plague and the Great Fire, Pepys recorded small details of everyday life, both private and public. In December 1663, he attended his first cockfight. His account of the evening at the cockpit in Shoe Lane, off Fleet Street, captures the atmosphere and action of this popular sport which remained legal until 1835. Pepys tells of the crowd's social mix, from 'Parliament-man ... to the poorest 'prentices', the cruelty of the sport, and the huge sums that people bet on it: the £20 loss he notes would have been about nine months' pay for a skilled workman.

from *Diary of Samuel Pepys*

Thence I on foot to Charing Crosse to the ordinary, and there dined, meeting Mr. Gauden and Creed. Here variety of talk but to no great purpose. After dinner won a wager of a payre of gloves of a crowne of Mr. Gauden upon some words in his contract for victualling. There parted in the street with them, and I to my Lord's, but he not being within, took coach, and, being directed by sight of bills upon the walls, I did go to Shoe Lane to see a cocke-fighting at a new pit there, a sport I was never at in my life; but, Lord! to see the strange variety of people, from Parliament-man (by name Wildes, that was Deputy Governor of the Tower when Robinson was Lord Mayor) to the poorest 'prentices, bakers, brewers, butchers, draymen, and what not; and all these fellows one with another in swearing, cursing, and betting. I soon had enough of it, and yet I would not but have seen it once, it being strange to observe the nature of these poor creatures, how they will fight till they drop down dead upon the table, and strike after they are ready to give up the ghost, not offering to run away when they are weary or wounded past doing further, whereas where a dunghill brood comes he will, after a sharp stroke that pricks him, run off the stage, and then they wring off his neck without more ado, whereas the other they preserve, though their eyes be both out, for breed only of a true cock of the game. Sometimes a cock that has had ten to one against him will by chance give an unlucky blow, will strike the other starke dead in a moment, that he never stirs more; but the common rule is, that though a cock neither runs nor dies, yet if any man will bet £10 to a crowne, and nobody take the bet, the game is given over, and not sooner. One thing more it is strange to see how people of this poor rank, that look as if they had not bread to put in their mouths, shall bet three or four pounds at one bet, and lose it, and yet bet as much the next battle (so they call every match of two cocks), so that one of them will lose £10 or £20 at a meeting.

DANIEL DEFOE
1660–1731

Daniel Defoe was a novelist, soldier, journalist and spy. As well as his famous novels, including *Robinson Crusoe* and *Moll Flanders*, he wrote many pamphlets on political and social questions, and a series of travelogues, published between 1724 and 1727 as *A Tour Thro' the Whole Island of Great Britain*. His observations on the social, business, and cultural life of the towns he visited serve as a wonderful introduction to the period. His visit to Newmarket takes us into the heart of horse racing. His detached account shows that it was not just a sport where all classes come together, but also a magnet for high rollers, cheats, and conmen. Defoe did take some pleasure in the races themselves, though, and his comparison to the Circus Maximus in ancient Rome conveys the thrill of a day at the races in Hanoverian England.

from *Tour Through the Eastern Counties of England*

Being come to Newmarket in the month of October, I had the opportunity to see the horse races and a great concourse of the nobility and gentry, as well from London as from all parts of England, but they were all so intent, so eager, so busy upon the sharping part of the sport—their wagers and bets—that to me they seemed just as so many horse-coursers in Smithfield, descending (the greatest of them) from their high dignity and quality to picking one another's pockets, and biting one another as much as possible, and that with such eagerness as that it might be said they acted without respect to faith, honour, or good manners.

There was Mr. Frampton the oldest, and, as some say, the cunningest jockey in England; one day he lost one thousand guineas, the next he won two thousand; and so alternately he made as light of throwing away five hundred or one thousand pounds at a time as other men do of their pocket-money, and as perfectly calm, cheerful, and unconcerned when he had lost one thousand pounds as when he had won it. On the other side there was Sir R. Fagg, of Sussex, of whom fame says he has the most in him and the least to show for it (relating to jockeyship) of any man there, yet he often carried the prize. His horses, they said, were all cheats, how honest soever their master was, for he scarce ever produced a horse but he looked like what he was not, and was what nobody could expect him to be. If he was as light as the wind, and could fly like a meteor, he was sure to look as clumsy, and as dirty, and as much like a cart-horse as all the cunning of his master and the grooms could make him, and just in this manner he beat some of the greatest gamesters in the field.

I was so sick of the jockeying part that I left the crowd about the posts and pleased myself with observing the horses: how the creatures yielded to all the arts and managements of their masters; how they took their airings in sport, and played with the daily heats which they ran over the course before the grand day. But how, as knowing the difference equally with their riders, would they exert their utmost strength at the time of the race itself! And that to such an extremity that one or two of them died in the stable when they came to be rubbed after the first heat.

Here I fancied myself in the Circus Maximus at Rome seeing the ancient games and the racings of the chariots and horsemen, and in this warmth of my imagination I pleased and diverted myself more and in a more noble manner than I could possibly do in the crowds of gentlemen at the weighing and starting-posts and at their coming in, or at their meetings at the coffee-houses and gaming-tables after the races were over, where there was little or nothing to be seen but what was the subject of just reproach to them and reproof from every wise man that looked upon them.

N.B.—Pray take it with you, as you go, you see no ladies at Newmarket, except a few of the neighbouring gentlemen's families, who come in their coaches on any particular day to see a race, and so go home again directly.

As I was pleasing myself with what was to be seen here, I went in the intervals of the sport to see the fine seats of the gentlemen in the neighbouring county, for this part of Suffolk, being an open champaign country and a healthy air, is formed for pleasure and all kinds of country diversion, Nature, as it were, inviting the gentlemen to visit her where she was fully prepared to receive them, in conformity to which kind summons they came, for the country is, as it were, covered with fine palaces of the nobility and pleasant seats of the gentlemen.

❧

FRANCES BURNEY
1752–1840

Frances Burney was an author whose satirical *Evelina* of 1778 was one of the earliest novels to be published by a woman in Britain. As well as her fiction and plays, she is celebrated as a diarist and letter-writer, with a style characterized by sharp observation of the mores of the upper-class world in which she moved. While staying in Devon in 1773, she wrote about the sports at Teignmouth. Alongside her witty descriptions of the flirtations and social networking indulged in by her party, Burney gives a detailed account of a seaside sporting festival, complete with cricket, races, a rowing match for women, and the 'most barbarous diversion' of a wrestling match. Her comparison between the Teignmouth races and the Olympiads, though tongue in cheek, suggests a growing interest in the ancient Olympics.

from *Diary of Fanny Burney*

I have not had a moment for writing this age—I never had less, as Mrs. R. and myself are almost inseparable. The Races, however, must by no means pass unrecorded.

Miss Lockwood and Miss Bowdler invited themselves to accompany us to the Race ground: Mr. Crispen also called in and joined us. Mr. Rishton was not at all pleased, and the half hour which we spent before we set out, he sat almost totally silent. Mr. Crispen addressed himself to me with his usual particularity, which really put me quite out of countenance, as I dreaded Miss Bowdler's opinion, and feared she would rank me with Miss Colbourne. I seated myself quietly at a distance, but Mr. Crispen, determined to torment me, drew his chair quite close to mine, and in so particular a manner that I could not keep my place but got up and seated myself next to Mrs. R. on the window.

I then wished that I had not, for every body (except Mr. R.) laughed: I felt my face on fire. "Do you run away from me," cried Mr. Crispen, "to take shelter under the Lamb?" But it was in vain, for he immediately moved after me, and continued, in the same style, to complain of me. I endeavoured to change the subject, and made some enquiries concerning the Races; but nothing would do. "Ah!" cried he, "would that your heart was to be run for! What an effort would I make!" "Yes," cried Miss Bowdler (not very delicately), "you would break your wind on the occasion, I doubt not." "What will they do," said I, "with the poor pig after the Races?" (one was to be run for).

"O that my heart," cried Mr. Crispen, "could be as easily cured!"

"Never fear," said Miss Bowdler, "it has stood a good many shocks!"

"Were it now to be opened," answered he, "you would find Burney engraved on it in large characters."

"O yes," cried she, "and you would find a great many pretty misses there besides!"

"Ay," said Mrs. R., "there would be Miss Colbourne."

"But Burney," cried he emphatically, "is my sum total. I own, I avow it publicly, I make no secret of it!"

"Yes, yes," returned Miss Bowdler, "the *Present* is always best!"

I just then recollected a little dispute which we had had with Mr. Rishton, on the pronunciation of some Italian words, and giving a grammar to Mr. Crispen, beg'd him to decide it.

"Look another way, my dear little Burney," cried he, "look another way—I must take out my reading glass!—You have a natural antipathy to me, but don't strengthen it by looking at me now!"

I was very glad when this conversation was concluded, by our being all obliged to march. We found a great deal of company, and a great deal of diversion. The sport began by an Ass Race. There were sixteen of the long eared tribe; some of them really ran extremely well; others were indeed truly ridiculous; but all of them diverting. Next followed a Pig Race. This was certainly cruel, for the poor animal had his tail cut to within the length of an inch, and then that inch was soaped. It was then let loose and made run. It was to be the property of the man who could catch it by the tail; which after many ridiculous attempts was found to be impossible, it was so very slippery. Therefore the candidates concluded this day's sport by running for it themselves. The great *Sweep Stakes* of the asses were half-a-guinea; the second prize a crown, and the third half-a-crown. However, the whole of it was truly laughable.

The next Race day was not till Friday, which day was also destined to a grand Cricket Match. Mr. Rishton is a very good player; and there is an excellent ground on the Den. Two gentlemen who were to be of the match breakfasted here in the morning. They are sons of Dr. Milles, Dean of Exeter ... The cricket players dined on the green, where they had a boothe erected, and a dinner from the Globe, the best Inn here, to which Mrs. Rishton added a *hash*, which Mr. T. Mills assured her was most excellent, for Mr. Hurrel himself eat three times of it! and that, he remarked, indisputably proved its goodness.

The Cricket Match was hardly over before the Tingmouth games began. All that was [to] be done this second day was Wrestling, a most barbarous diversion, and which I could not look on, and would not have gone to if I had not feared being thought affected. A ring was formed for the combattants by a rope railing, from which we stood to see the sport!! The wrestler was to conquer twice, one opponent immediately after another, to entitle himself to the prize. A strong labouring man came off victorious in the first battles; but while his shins were yet bleeding, he was obliged to attack another. The hat (their gauntlet) was thrown by a servant of Mr. Colbourn's. He was reckoned by the judges an admirable wrestler, and he very fairly beat his adversary. A sailor directly flung his hat: he was sworn friend of the defeated labourer. He entered the lists in a passion, and attacked the servant, as all the gentlemen said, very unfairly, and, while a short truce was declared for the man to have his shoe unbuckled, he very dishonourably hit him a violent blow. Upon this they both prepared for a boxing match, and were upon the point of engaging (though the whole Ring cried out "shame" upon the sailor), when Mr. Rishton inflamed with generous rage at this foul play, rushed precipitately into the Ring, and getting between the combattants, collared the sailor, declaring he should be turned out of the lists.

I am really amazed that he escaped being ill-treated; but, at the very instant, two of the young Mills ran into the Ring and catching hold of Mr. Rishton insisted on his not venturing himself against the brutality of the enraged sailor. However, he would not retire till the sailor was voted out of the lists as a foul player. Mr. Rishton then returned to us between the Mr. Mills. Every body seemed in admiration of the spirit which he exerted on this occasion.

The Tingmouth Games concluded the day after with a Rowing Match between the women of Shaldon, a fishing town on the other side of the Ting, and the fair ones of this place. For all the men are at Newfoundland every summer, and all laborious work is done by the women, who have a strength and hardiness which I have never seen before in our race.

The following morning, while Mrs. R. and myself were dressing, we received a very civil message from Mrs. and Miss Colbourne to invite us to see the rowing in their carriage. Mrs. R. sent word that we would come to them on the Den; but afterwards we recollected that we were engaged to tea at Mrs. Phips. This put us in a dilemma; but as Mrs. Phips's was the prior engagement, we were obliged to march to Mr.Colbourne's coach on the Den to make our apologies. The first object I saw was Mr. Crispen. He expressed himself prodigiously charmed at seeing us. I said we were obliged [to go. He] said he had heard of our not being well—"I could ill bear," he added, "to hear of the Lamb's illness—but when they told me that *you* was not well!—I should not have been so long without seeing you, but from having had a violent cold and fever myself—[and I] thought in my confinement that one half hour's conversation with you would completely recover me."

"If I had known," said I, "my miraculous power—"

"O," cried he, taking my hand, "it is not yet too late! If you are mercifully disposed."—I skipt off.

We made our apologies as well as we could, and they insisted on setting us down at Mr. Phips', Mrs. Colbourn and Mr. Crispen on one side and we three lasses on the other. All the way we went Mr. Crispen amused himself with holding the same kind of language to me, notwithstanding the presence of Miss Colbourne.

The women rowed with astonishing dexterity and quickness. There were five boats of them. The prizes which they won were, shifts with pink ribbands. Games such as these, Mr. Crispen says, ought to make future events be dated as universally from Tingmothiads as former ones were from Olympiads.

RICHARD GRAVES
1715–1804

Anglican clergyman Richard Graves published
novels and poetry. His most famous novel was *The
Spiritual Quixote* (1773), a satirical story of a deluded
man's journey that made a nod to Cervantes's classic *Don Quixote*. Instead of the Spanish knight and
his sidekick, Sancho Panza, in the original, Graves's
fictional hero was a Methodist preacher, Geoffry
Wildgoose, who, with Jerry Tugwell in the Panza
role, travelled around England attempting to save
people's souls. In this extract, they arrive at the
Cotswold Olimpicks, famous for their boozy atmosphere, boisterous games, and the anti-puritanical
attitudes of the crowd. Wildgoose's impromptu
sermon decrying what he saw as the sinful sports of
smock racing and wrestling does not win any con-
verts. Indeed, the crowd make it very clear what they
think of his attempts to disrupt their fun with his
preaching.

from *The Spiritual Quixote*

They now approached the place of rendezvous, where the revel was held, which was a large plain on the Cotswold-hills. Their ears were saluted with a confused noise of drums, trumpets, and whistle-pipes; not those martial sounds, however, which are heard in the field of battle, but such as those harmless instruments emit, with which children amuse themselves in a country fair. There was a great number of swains in their holiday-clothes, with their belts and silk handkerchiefs; and nymphs in straw hats and tawdry ribbands, flaunting, ogling and coquetting (in their rustic way) with as much alacrity as any of the gay flutterers in the Mall.

A ring was formed about the wrestlers and cudgel-players, by the substantial farmers on their long-tailed steeds, and two or three forlorn coaches sauntering about with their vapourish possessors; who crept out from their neighbouring seats, to contemplate the humours of these awkward rustics, and waste an hour of their tedious month in the country, where, as a great modern observes, 'small matters serve for amusement.'

Wildgoose and his friend Jerry, making but a small figure in this humorous assembly, were at a loss how to draw the attention of the multitude. As they had made a dry breakfast, and had drunk nothing the whole day, Jerry asked his master, 'Whether it were any sin, to call for a pint of ale, at sich a time as this?' So, with Wildgoose's consent, they went to one of the booths, and were refreshing themselves with the foresaid potation, when the company began to divide; and proclamation was made, that a holland shift, which was adorned with ribbands, and displayed on a pole, was going to be run for, and six young women began to exhibit themselves before the whole assembly, in a dress hardly reconcileable to the rules of decency.

'Nice people have been observed to have the grossest ideas;' and, perhaps, such chaste men have the most unchaste conceptions of things. Be that as it will, Wildgoose no sooner perceived that mysterious veil of modesty, the holland smock, thus rudely exposed to public view, and these young women prepared to engage in so loose a diversion, than he found his wonted zeal revive; and mounting upon an inverted hamper, near the booth, he beckoned to the mob, crying out,

'For Christ's sake, my Christian brethren, if you have any regard to the health of your souls, desist from these anti-christian, these more than paganish recreations, which are poison, and listen to my words.'

The people, seeing a man of a tolerable appearance thus exalted above the crowd, and preparing to harangue, began to stare, and to enquire of each other what he would be at! As they heard imperfectly the word 'health,' and more words of a medicinal tendency, the prevailing opinion was, that a mountebank was going to dispense his medicines, for the benefit of mankind; and Tugwell's wallet was supposed to contain the sovereign packet of the learned doctor. Mr. Wildgoose, however, soon undeceived them, by addressing the crowd in the apostolical style; though he had not yet acquired the true bon ton or Gospel lingo of Mr. Whitfield and his associates.

'Men, brethren, and fellow-christians! You are here assembled to keep holiday! that is, to sacrifice to the Devil; to perform the most agreeable service, which you could possibly devise, to that enemy of mankind.

'This festival is called Whitsuntide, and was appointed to commemorate the most solemn event recorded in the annals of our religion; namely, the effusion of the Holy Spirit upon the primitive apostles. But instead of being filled with the Holy Spirit, as the apostles were, you are filling yourselves with spirituous liquors and strong drink; with the spirits of geneva, with English spirits, and foreign spirits, and what not!

'Oh! my brethren, consider what you are about; is this renouncing the Devil and all his works? Is this despising the pomps and vanities of this wicked world? and resisting the sinful lusts of the flesh? The very purpose and intent of this ungodly meeting is directly opposite to your most solemn vow at your baptism. Instead of guarding yourselves against the attacks of your spiritual adversary, instead of bruising the head of that old serpent, the Devil; you are breaking one another's heads with cudgels and quarter-staffs; instead of wrestling against flesh and blood, you are wrestling with and supplanting one another. So far from renouncing the pomps and vanities of this wicked world, you are running for holland smocks, and making provision for the lusts of the flesh.

'Ah! my dear country-women, you that are so solicitous for these terrestrial garments, these garments spotted by the flesh! let me beseech you to labour after the celestial robes, the spiritual decorations and saint-like ornaments of piety, meekness, and chastity; and not to set your hearts upon such profane trappings as pink ribbands and holland smocks.

'Indeed, what use will you make of these tawdry shifts, should you gain the prize! I blush to answer such a question. They may make a poor *shift*, like the fig-leaves of Eve, to cover the nakedness of your bodies, as our good works do the nakedness of our souls. But unless you are clothed with a better righteousness than your own, you will hereafter be stripped bare, and be exposed to the derision of men and angels—'

From the secret connexion which this subject had with generation, Mr. Wildgoose was insensibly sliding into the nature of regeneration, and the new-birth; and was going to explain some of the most mysterious doctrines of Christianity to these unruly disciples, when a good orthodox publican, thinking his craft was in danger, cried out, 'Odzounterkins! lift up the smock! come, my maids! stand ready for the sport!'

He was seconded by a shrewd young carter, with a silk handkerchief about his neck, who could not but laugh at the familiarity of Wildgoose's comparisons; and thinking also that this harangue would spoil the diversion, which they were now intent upon, he threw the rind of an orange at the orator's head. Another levelled a piece of horse-dung, with an unlucky dexterity, exactly into Tugwell's mouth as he stood listening with a conceited attention to his master's eloquence. Their example was followed by a great part of the company; who, as Jerry had foretold, began to bombard them so furiously with clods of dirt and horse-dung, that Mr. Wildgoose was soon forced to dismount from the top of his hamper: and one of them, tilting up the form on which Tugwell was exalted, laid him sprawling in the moisture occasioned by the staling of horses, or spilling of the liquor; where he lay wallowing for some time, being saluted with several bumps and jostles in contrary directions, which prevented his emerging from the slippery soil.

In short, Wildgoose thought it advisable to preserve himself for a more favourable opportunity; wherefore, lifting up and disengaging his fellow-labourer, they drew off from the field of battle, amidst the loud scoffs and exulting shouts of the unthinking multitude; Wildgoose only expressing his compassion for them by a significant shake of the head, and crying out, 'Poor souls! they know not what they do:' and Jerry, when he was got pretty well out of their reach, bawled out, 'Ay! ay! parsecute on—parsecute on—parsecute—parsecute! You have the best of it in this world, but we shall be even with you in the next.'

JANE AUSTEN
1775–1817

In her novels, Jane Austen explores the social networks of the aristocracy and rising middle classes. Her heroines in *Emma*, *Mansfield Park*, *Pride and Prejudice* and more negotiate their families' expectations of marriage, property, and propriety. In *Northanger Abbey*, published posthumously in 1818, Austen tells the story of young Catherine Morland, a lively heroine with an overactive imagination and a love of Gothic novels. In this extract from Chapter 1, we see Catherine's playful childhood and early teens spent enjoying sport and games rather than studying. For modern audiences, this extract reminds us of the long history of women's cricket and of baseball as a game played by English children long before it evolved into an all-American sport.

Writing and accounts she was taught by her father; French by her mother: her proficiency in either was not remarkable, and she shirked her lessons in both whenever she could. What a strange, unaccountable character!—for with all these symptoms of profligacy at ten years old, she had neither a bad heart nor a bad temper; was seldom stubborn, scarcely ever quarrelsome, and very kind to the little ones, with few interruptions of tyranny; she was moreover noisy and wild, hated confinement and cleanliness, and loved nothing so well in the world as rolling down the green slope at the back of the house.

Such was Catherine Morland at ten. At fifteen, appearances were mending; she began to curl her hair and long for balls; her complexion improved, her features were softened by plumpness and colour, her eyes gained more animation, and her figure more consequence. Her love of dirt gave way to an inclination for finery, and she grew clean as she grew smart; she had now the pleasure of sometimes hearing her father and mother remark on her personal improvement. "Catherine grows quite a good-looking girl,—she is almost pretty to day," were words which caught her ears now and then; and how welcome were the sounds! To look *almost* pretty, is an acquisition of higher delight to a girl who has been looking plain the first fifteen years of her life, than a beauty from her cradle can ever receive.

Mrs. Morland was a very good woman, and wished to see her children every thing they ought to be; but her time was so much occupied in lying-in and teaching the little ones, that her elder daughters were inevitably left to shift for themselves; and it was not very wonderful that Catherine, who had by nature nothing heroic about her, should prefer cricket, base ball, riding on horseback, and running about the country at the age of fourteen, to books—or at least books of information—for, provided that nothing like useful knowledge could be gained from them, provided they were all story and no reflection, she had never any objection to books at all. But from fifteen to seventeen she was in training for a heroine; she read all such works as heroines must read to supply their memories with those quotations which are so serviceable and so soothing in the vicissitudes of their eventful lives.

WALTER SCOTT
1771–1832

Prolific author Walter Scott is widely acclaimed as a pioneer of historical novels. In *Ivanhoe*, published in 1819, he explores power and chivalry in twelfth century England. The novel helped to launch a cult of medieval romance that lasted throughout the nineteenth century. Its famous tournament sequence gave Scott a chance to play out his story about rival families against a romantic backdrop of jousting and melees, complete with mysterious knights. This extract covers the tournament's climax as Robin of Locksley – aka Robin Hood – takes on Prince John's favourites in the archery competition. Scott captures the excitement of the match, and his historical research on medieval archery shines through in every detail.

from *Ivanhoe*

The sound of the trumpets soon recalled those spectators who had already begun to leave the field; and proclamation was made that Prince John, suddenly called by high and peremptory public duties, held himself obliged to discontinue the entertainments of tomorrow's festival: nevertheless, that, unwilling so many good yeomen should depart without a trial of skill, he was pleased to appoint them, before leaving the ground, presently to execute the competition of archery intended for the morrow. To the best archer, a prize was to be awarded, being a bugle-horn, mounted with silver, and a silken baldric richly ornamented with a medallion of Saint Hubert, the patron of silvan sport.

More than thirty yeomen at first presented themselves as competitors, several of whom were rangers and underkeepers in the royal forests of Needwood and Charnwood. When, however, the archers understood with whom they were to be matched, upwards of twenty withdrew themselves from the contest, unwilling to encounter the dishonour of almost certain defeat. For in those days the skill of each celebrated marksman was as well known for many miles round him, as the qualities of a horse trained at Newmarket are familiar to those who frequent that well-known meeting.

The diminished list of competitors for silvan fame still amounted to eight. Prince John stepped from his royal seat to view more nearly the persons of these chosen yeomen, several of whom wore the royal livery. Having satisfied his curiosity by this investigation, he looked for the object of his resentment, whom he observed standing on the same spot, and with the same composed countenance which he had exhibited upon the preceding day.

"Fellow," said Prince John, "I guessed by thy insolent babble thou wert no true lover of the longbow, and I see thou darest not adventure thy skill among such merry-men as stand yonder."

"Under favour, sir," replied the yeoman, "I have another reason for refraining to shoot, besides the fearing discomfiture and disgrace."

"And what is thy other reason?" said Prince John, who, for some cause which perhaps he could not himself have explained, felt a painful curiosity respecting this individual.

"Because," replied the woodsman, "I know not if these yeomen and I are used to shoot at the same marks; and because, moreover, I know not how your Grace might relish the winning of a third prize by one who has unwittingly fallen under your displeasure."

Prince John coloured as he put the question, "What is thy name, yeoman?"

"Locksley," answered the yeoman.

"Then, Locksley," said Prince John, "thou shalt shoot in thy turn, when these yeomen have displayed their skill. If thou carriest the prize, I will add to it twenty nobles; but if thou losest it, thou shalt be stript of thy Lincoln green, and scourged out of the lists with bowstrings, for a wordy and insolent braggart."

"And how if I refuse to shoot on such a wager?" said the yeoman.—"Your Grace's power, supported, as it is, by so many men-at-arms, may indeed easily strip and scourge me, but cannot compel me to bend or to draw my bow."

"If thou refusest my fair proffer," said the Prince, "the Provost of the lists shall cut thy bow-string, break thy bow and arrows, and expel thee from the presence as a faint-hearted craven."

"This is no fair chance you put on me, proud Prince," said the yeoman," to compel me to peril myself against the best archers of Leicester and Staffordshire, under the penalty of infamy if they should overshoot me. Nevertheless, I will obey your pleasure."

"Look to him close, men-at-arms," said Prince John, "his heart is sinking; I am jealous lest he attempt to escape the trial.—And do you, good fellows, shoot boldly round; a buck and a butt of wine are ready for your refreshment in yonder tent, when the prize is won."

A target was placed at the upper end of the southern avenue which led to the lists. The contending archers took their station in turn, at the bottom of the southern access; the distance between that station and the mark allowing full distance for what was called a shot at rovers. The archers, having previously determined by lot their order of precedence, were to shoot each three shafts in succession. The sports were regulated by an officer of inferior rank, termed the Provost of the Games; for the high rank of the marshals of the lists would have been held degraded, had they condescended to superintend the sports of the yeomanry.

One by one the archers, stepping forward, delivered their shafts yeomanlike and bravely. Of twenty-four arrows, shot in succession, ten were fixed in the target, and the others ranged so near it, that, considering the distance of the mark, it was accounted good archery. Of the ten shafts which hit the target, two within the inner ring were shot by

Hubert, a forester in the service of Malvoisin, who was accordingly pronounced victorious.

"Now, Locksley," said Prince John to the bold yeoman, with a bitter smile, "wilt thou try conclusions with Hubert, or wilt thou yield up bow, baldric, and quiver, to the Provost of the sports?"

"Sith it be no better," said Locksley, "I am content to try my fortune; on condition that when I have shot two shafts at yonder mark of Hubert's, he shall be bound to shoot one at that which I shall propose."

"That is but fair," answered Prince John, "and it shall not be refused thee.—If thou dost beat this braggart, Hubert, I will fill the bugle with silver pennies for thee."

"A man can do but his best," answered Hubert; "but my grandsire drew a good long-bow at Hastings, and I trust not to dishonour his memory."

The former target was now removed, and a fresh one of the same size placed in its room. Hubert, who, as victor in the first trial of skill, had the right to shoot first, took his aim with great deliberation, long measuring the distance with his eye, while he held in his hand his bended bow, with the arrow placed on the string. At length he made a step forward, and raising the bow at the full stretch of his left arm, till the centre or grasping-place was nigh level with his face, he drew his bow-string to his ear. The arrow whistled through the air, and lighted within the inner ring of the target, but not exactly in the centre.

"You have not allowed for the wind, Hubert," said his antagonist, bending his bow, "or that had been a better shot."

So saying, and without shewing the least anxiety to pause upon his aim, Locksley stept to the appointed station, and shot his arrow as carelessly in appearance as if he had not even looked at the mark. He was speaking almost at the instant that the shaft left the bow-string, yet it alighted in the target two inches nearer to the white spot which marked the centre than that of Hubert.

"By the light of Heaven!" said Prince John to Hubert, "an thou suffer that runagate knave to overcome thee, thou art worthy of the gallows!"

Hubert had but one set speech for all occasions. "An your highness were to hang me," he said, "a man can but do his best. Nevertheless, my grandsire drew a good bow—"

"The foul fiend on thy grandsire and all his generation!" interrupted John; "shoot, knave, and shoot thy best, or it shall be worse for thee!"

Thus exhorted, Hubert resumed his place, and not neglecting the caution which he had received from his adversary, he made the necessary allowance for a very light air of wind, which had just arisen, and shot so successfully that his arrow alighted in the very centre of the target.

"A Hubert! a Hubert!" shouted the populace, more interested in a known person than in a stranger. "In the clout!—in the clout!—a Hubert for ever!"

"Thou canst not mend that shot, Locksley," said the Prince with an insulting smile.

"I will notch his shaft for him, however," replied Locksley.

And letting fly his arrow with a little more precaution than before, it lighted right upon that of his competitor, which it split to shivers. The people who stood around were so astonished at his wonderful dexterity, that they could not even give vent to their surprise in their usual clamour. "This must be the devil, and no man of flesh and blood," whispered the yeomen to each other; "such archery was never seen since a bow was first bent in Britain."

"And now," said Locksley, "I will crave your Grace's permission to plant such a mark as is used in the North Country; and welcome every brave yeoman who shall try a shot at it to win a smile from the bonny lass he loves best."

He then turned to leave the lists. "Let your guards attend me," he said, "if you please—I go but to cut a rod from the next willow-bush."

Prince John made a signal that some attendants should follow him in case of his escape; but the cry of "Shame! shame!" which burst from the multitude, induced him to alter his ungenerous purpose.

"Locksley returned almost instantly with a willow wand about six feet in length, perfectly straight, and rather thicker than a man's thumb. He began to peel this with great composure, observing at the same time, that to ask a good woodsman to shoot at a target so broad as had hitherto been used, was to put shame upon his skill. "For his own part," he said, "and in the land where he was bred, men would as soon take for their mark King Arthur's round table, which held sixty Knights around it. A child of seven years old," he said, "might hit yonder target with a headless shaft; but," added he, walking deliberately to the other end of the lists, and sticking the willow wand upright in the ground, "he that hits that rod at five-score yards, I call him an archer fit to bear both bow and quiver before a king, an it were the stout King Richard himself."

"My grandsire," said Hubert, "drew a good bow at the battle of Hastings, and never shot at such a mark in his life—and neither will I. If this yeoman can cleave that rod, I give him the bucklers—or rather, I yield to the devil that is in his jerkin, and not to any human skill; a man can but do his best, and I will not shoot where I am sure to miss. I might as well shoot at the edge of our parson's whittle, or at a wheat straw, or at a sunbeam, as at a twinkling white streak which I can hardly see."

"Cowardly dog!" said Prince John.—"Sirrah Locksley, do thou shoot; but, if thou hittest such a mark, I will say thou art the first man ever did so. Howe'er it be, thou shalt not crow over us with a mere show of superior skill."

"I will do my best, as Hubert says," answered Locksley; "no man can do more."

So saying, he again bent his bow, but on the present occasion looked with attention to his weapon, and changed the string, which he thought was no longer truly round, having been a little frayed by the two former shots. He then took his aim with some deliberation, and the multitude awaited the event in breathless silence. The archer vindicated their opinion of his skill: his arrow split the willow rod against which it was aimed. A jubilee of acclamations followed; and even Prince John, in admiration of Locksley's skill, lost for an instant his dislike to his person. "These twenty nobles," he said, "which, with the bugle, thou hast fairly won, are thine own; we will make them fifty, if thou wilt take livery and service with us as a yeoman of our body guard, and be near to our person. For never did so strong a hand bend a bow, or so true an eye direct a shaft."

"Pardon me, noble Prince," said Locksley; "but I have vowed, that if ever I take service, it should be with your royal brother, King Richard. These twenty nobles I leave to Hubert, who has this day drawn as brave a bow as his grandsire did at Hastings. Had his modesty not refused the trial, he would have hit the wand as well as I."

Hubert shook his head as he received with reluctance the bounty of the stranger; and Locksley, anxious to escape farther observation, mixed with the crowd, and was seen no more.

WILLIAM HAZLITT
1778–1830

William Hazlitt was a journalist, art critic, and essayist, who was as at home amongst the Romantic poets as he was in 'the Fancy', the fashionable sporting world that centred on horseracing, betting, and pugilism. His essay 'The Fight', published in 1822, is one of the best descriptions we have of an illegal prize fight from Regency England. Bill Neate and 'the Gasman', Tom Hickman, fought it out on Hungerford Common in December 1821. Hazlitt captures everything about the fight: the social mix of 'swells' and 'rustics' in the huge crowd, the importance of the bookmakers and the experts from the Fancy in assessing the fighters, and, of course, the action itself. The visceral writing captures the blood and brutality of 'a good stand-up fight'. Two centuries on, 'The Fight' remains a masterpiece in sports writing.

from 'The Fight'

Reader, have you ever seen a fight? If not, you have a pleasure to come, at least if it is a fight like that between the Gas-man and Bill Neate. The crowd was very great when we arrived on the spot; open carriages were coming up, with streamers flying and music playing, and the country-people were pouring in over hedge and ditch in all directions, to see their hero beat or be beaten. The odds were still on Gas, but only about five to four. Gully had been down to try Neate, and had backed him considerably, which was a damper to the sanguine confidence of the adverse party. About two hundred thousand pounds were pending. The Gas says, he has lost 3000*l*. which were promised him by different gentlemen if he had won. He had presumed too much on himself, which had made others presume on him. This spirited and formidable young fellow seems to have taken for his motto the old maxim, that 'there are three things necessary to success in life—*Impudence! Impudence! Impudence!*' It is so in matters of opinion, but not in the *Fancy*, which is the most practical of all things, though even here confidence is half the battle, but only half. Our friend had vapoured and swaggered too much, as if he wanted to grin and bully his adversary out of the fight. 'Alas! the Bristol man was not so tamed!'—'This is *the grave-digger*' (would Tom Hickman exclaim in the moments of intoxication from gin and success, shewing his tremendous right hand), 'this will send many of them to their long homes; I haven't done with them yet!' Why should he—though he had licked four of the best men within the hour, yet why should he threaten to inflict dishonourable chastisement on my old master Richmond, a veteran going off the stage, and who has borne his sable honours meekly? Magnanimity, my dear Tom, and bravery, should be inseparable. Or why should he go up to his antagonist, the first time he ever saw him at the Fives Court, and measuring him from head to foot with a glance of contempt, as Achilles surveyed Hector, say to him, 'What, are you Bill Neate? I'll knock more blood out of that great carcase of thine, this day fortnight, than you ever knock'd out of a bullock's!' It was not manly, 'twas not fighter-like. If he was sure of the victory (as he was not), the less said about it the better. Modesty should accompany the *Fancy* as its shadow. The best men were always the best behaved. Jem Belcher, the Game Chicken (before whom the Gas-man could not have lived), were civil, silent men. So is Cribb, so is Tom Belcher, the most elegant of sparrers, and not a man for every one to take

46

by the nose. I enlarged on this topic in the mail (while Turtle was asleep), and said very wisely (as I thought) that impertinence was a part of no profession. A boxer was bound to beat his man, but not to thrust his fist, either actually or by implication, in every one's face. Even a highwayman, in the way of trade, may blow out your brains, but if he uses foul language at the same time, I should say he was no gentleman. A boxer, I would infer, need not be a blackguard or a coxcomb, more than another. Perhaps I press this point too much on a fallen man—Mr Thomas Hickman has by this time learnt that first of all lessons, 'That man was made to mourn.' He has lost nothing by the late fight but his presumption; and that every man may do as well without! By an over-display of this quality, however, the public had been prejudiced against him, and the *knowing-ones* were taken in. Few but those who had bet on him wished Gas to win. With my own prepossessions on the subject, the result of the IIth of December appeared to me as fine a piece of poetical justice as I had ever witnessed. The difference of weight between the two combatants (14 stone to 12) was nothing to the sporting men. Great, heavy, clumsy, long-armed Bill Neate kicked the beam in the scale of the Gas-man's vanity. The amateurs were frightened at his big words, and thought that they would make up for the difference of six feet and five feet nine. Truly, the *Fancy* are not men of imagination. They judge of what has been, and cannot conceive of any thing that is to be. The Gasman had won hitherto; therefore he must beat a man half as big again as himself—and that to a certainty. Besides, there are as many feuds, factions, prejudices, pedantic notions in the *Fancy* as in the state or in the schools. Mr Gully is almost the only cool, sensible man among them, who exercises an unbiassed discretion, and is not a slave to his passions in these matters. But enough of reflections, and to our tale. The day, as I have said, was fine for a December morning. The grass was wet, and the ground miry, and ploughed up with multitudinous feet, except that, within the ring itself, there was a spot of virgin-green closed in and unprofaned by vulgar tread, that shone with dazzling brightness in the mid-day sun. For it was now noon, and we had an hour to wait. This is the trying time. It is then the heart sickens, as you think what the two champions are about, and how short a time will determine their fate. After the first blow is struck, there is no opportunity for nervous apprehensions; you are swallowed up in the immediate interest of the scene—but

Between the acting of a dreadful thing
And the first motion, all the interim is
Like a phantasma, or a hideous dream.

I found it so as I felt the sun's rays clinging to my back, and saw the white wintry clouds sink below the verge of the horizon. 'So, I thought, my fairest hopes have faded from my sight!—so will the Gas-man's glory, or that of his adversary, vanish in an hour.' The *swells* were parading in their white box-coats, the outer ring was cleared with some bruises on the heads and shins of the rustic assembly (for the *cockneys* had been distanced by the sixty-six miles); the time drew near, I had got a good stand; a bustle, a buzz, ran through the crowd, and from the opposite side entered Neate, between his second and bottle-holder. He rolled along, swathed in his loose great coat, his knock-knees bending under his huge bulk; and, with a modest cheerful air, threw his hat into the ring. He then just looked round, and began quietly to undress; when from the other side there was a similar rush and an opening made, and the Gas-man came forward with a conscious air of anticipated triumph, too much like the cock-of-the-walk. He strutted about more than became a hero, sucked oranges with a supercilious air, and threw away the skin with a toss of his head, and went up

and looked at Neate, which was an act of super-
erogation. The only sensible thing he did was, as he
strode away from the modern Ajax, to fling out his
arms, as if he wanted to try whether they would do
their work that day. By this time they had stripped,
and presented a strong contrast in appearance. If
Neate was like Ajax, 'with Atlantean shoulders, fit to
bear' the pugilistic reputation of all Bristol, Hickman might be compared to Diomed, light, vigorous,
elastic, and his back glistened in the sun, as he
moved about, like a panther's hide. There was now
a dead pause—attention was awe-struck. Who at
that moment, big with a great event, did not draw
his breath short—did not feel his heart throb? All
was ready. They tossed up for the sun, and the Gas-
man won. They were led up to the *scratch*—shook
hands, and went at it.

In the first round every one thought it was all
over. After making play a short time, the Gas-man
flew at his adversary like a tiger, struck five blows in
as many seconds, three first, and then following him
as he staggered back, two more, right and left, and
down he fell, a mighty ruin. There was a shout, and I
said, 'There is no standing this.' Neate seemed like a
lifeless lump of flesh and bone, round which the Gas-
man's blows played with the rapidity of electricity or
lightning, and you imagined he would only be lifted

up to be knocked down again. It was as if Hickman held a sword or a fire in that right hand of his, and directed it against an unarmed body. They met again, and Neate seemed, not cowed, but particularly cautious. I saw his teeth clenched together and his brows knit close against the sun. He held out both his arms at full length straight before him, like two sledgehammers, and raised his left an inch or two higher. The Gas-man could not get over this guard—they struck mutually and fell, but without advantage on either side. It was the same in the next round; but the balance of power was thus restored—the fate of the battle was suspended. No one could tell how it would end. This was the only moment in which opinion was divided; for, in the next, the Gas-man aiming a mortal blow at his adversary's neck, with his right hand, and failing from the length he had to reach, the other returned it with his left at full swing, planted a tremendous blow on his cheek-bone and eyebrow, and made a red ruin of that side of his face. The Gas-man went down, and there was another shout—a roar of triumph as the waves of fortune rolled tumultuously from side to side. This was a settler. Hickman got up, and 'grinned horrible a ghastly smile,' yet he was evidently dashed in his opinion of himself; it was the first time he had ever been so punished; all one side of his face was perfect scarlet, and his right eye was closed in dingy blackness, as he advanced to the fight, less confident, but still determined. After one or two rounds, not receiving another such remembrancer, he rallied and went at it with his former impetuosity. But in vain. His strength had been weakened,—his blows could not tell at such a distance,—he was obliged to fling himself at his adversary, and could not strike from his feet; and almost as regularly as he flew at him with his right hand, Neate warded the blow, or drew back out of its reach, and felled him with the return of his left. There was little cautious sparring—no half-hits—no tapping and trifling, none of the *petit-maitreship* of the art—they were almost all knock-down blows:—the fight was a good stand-up fight. The wonder was the half-minute time. If there had been a minute or more allowed between each round, it would have been intelligible how they should by degrees recover strength and resolution; but to see two men smashed to the ground, smeared with gore, stunned, senseless, the breath beaten out of their bodies; and then, before you recover from the shock, to see them rise up with new strength and courage, stand steady to inflict or receive mortal offence, and rush upon each other 'like two clouds over the Caspian'—this is the most astonishing thing of all:—this is the high and heroic state of man! From this time

52

forward the event became more certain every round; and about the twelfth it seemed as if it must have been over. Hickman generally stood with his back to me; but in the scuffle, he had changed positions, and Neate just then made a tremendous lunge at him, and hit him full in the face. It was doubtful whether he would fall backwards or forwards; he hung suspended for a second or two, and then fell back, throwing his hands in the air, and with his face lifted up to the sky. I never saw any thing more terrific than his aspect just before he fell. All traces of life, of natural expression, were gone from him. His face was like a human skull, a death's head, spouting blood. The eyes were filled with blood, the nose streamed with blood, the mouth gaped blood. He was not like an actual man, but like a preternatural, spectral appearance, or like one of the figures in Dante's *Inferno*. Yet he fought on after this for several rounds, still striking the first desperate blow, and Neate standing on the defensive, and using the same cautious guard to the last, as if he had still all his work to do; and it was not till the Gas-man was so stunned in the seventeenth or eighteenth round, that his senses forsook him, and he could not come to time, that the battle was declared over. Ye who despise the *Fancy*, do something to shew as much *pluck*, or as much self-possession as this, before you assume a superiority which you have never given a single proof of by any one action in the whole course of your lives!—When the Gas-man came to himself, the first words he uttered were, 'Where am I? What is the matter?' 'Nothing is the matter, Tom,—you have lost the battle, but you are the bravest man alive.' And Jackson whispered to him, 'I am collecting a purse for you, Tom.'—Vain sounds, and unheard at that moment! Neate instantly went up and shook him cordially by the hand, and seeing some old acquaintance, began to flourish with his fists, calling out, 'Ah you always said I couldn't fight—What do you think now?' But all in good humour, and without any appearance of arrogance; only it was evident Bill Neate was pleased that he had won the fight. When it was over, I asked Cribb if he did not think it was a good one? He said, '*Pretty well!*' The carrier-pigeons now mounted into the air, and one of them flew with the news of her husband's victory to the bosom of Mrs Neate. Alas, for Mrs Hickman!

WILLIAM COBBETT
1763–1835

William Cobbett was a journalist, author, and Member of Parliament who advocated both parliamentary and economic reform over a long and varied career. In *Rural Rides*, published between 1822 and 1826, he explored the social and economic condition of the countryside in southern England and the Midlands. Sport, in the form of hunting, shooting, and fishing, naturally played a part in this critical survey; as he writes in this extract, 'the great business of life, in the country, appertains ... to the *game*'. Shooting was integral to social life in the country, and in this account Cobbett exposes the cheating to which some men would stoop in order to appear as better shots than they really were. Cobbett's friend bragging about how many partridges he bagged reminds us of the angler's tale of the fabled 'one that got away'. Self-aggrandizement and exaggeration have evidently been features of sport for centuries.

from *Rural Rides*

The great business of life, in the country, appertains, in some way or other, to the *game*, and especially at this time of the year. If it were not for the game, a country life would be like an *everlasting honey-moon*, which would, in about, half a century, put an end to the human race. In *towns*, or large villages, people make a shift to find the means of rubbing the rust off from each other by a vast variety of sources of contest. A couple of wives meeting in the street, and giving each other a wry look, or a look not quite civil enough, will, if the parties be hard pushed for a ground of contention, do pretty well. But in the country, there is, alas! no such resource. Here are no walls for people to take of each other. Here they are so placed as to prevent the possibility of such lucky local contact. Here is more than room of every sort, elbow, leg, horse, or carriage, for them all. Even *at Church* (most of the people being in the meeting-houses) the pews are surprisingly too large. Here, therefore, where all circumstances seem calculated to cause never-ceasing concord with its accompanying dullness, there would be no relief at all, were it not for the *game*. This, happily, supplies the place of all other sources of alternate dispute and reconciliation; it keeps all in life and motion, from the lord down to the hedger. When I see two men, whether in a market-room, by the way-side, in a parlour, in a church yard, or even in the church itself, engaged in manifestly deep and most momentous discourse, I will, if it be any time between September and February, bet *ten to one*, that it is, in some way or other, about *the game*. The wives and daughters hear so much of it, that they inevitably get engaged in the disputes; and thus all are kept in a state of vivid animation. I should like very much to be able to take a spot, a circle of 12 miles in diameter, and take an exact account of all the *time* spent by each individual, above the age of *ten* (that is the age they begin at), in *talking*, during the game season of one year, about *the game* and about *sporting exploits*. I verily believe that it would amount, upon an average, to *six times* as much as *all the other talk put together*; and, as to the *anger*, the *satisfaction*, the *scolding*, the *commendation*, the *chagrin*, the *exultation*, the *envy*, the *emulation*, where are there any of these in the country, unconnected with *the game*?

There is, however, an important distinction to be made between *hunters* (including coursers) and *shooters*. The latter are, as far as relates to their exploits, a disagreeable class, compared with the former; and the reason of this is, their doings are almost wholly *their own*; while, in the case of the others, the achievements are the property of *the dogs*. Nobody likes to hear another talk *much* in praise of his own acts, unless those acts have a manifest tendency to produce some good to the hearer; and shooters do talk *much* of their own exploits, and those exploits rather tend to *humiliate* the hearer. Then, a *great shooter* will, nine times out of ten, go so far as almost to *lie a little*; and, though people do not tell him of it, they do not like him the better for it; and he but too frequently discovers that they do not believe him: whereas, hunters are mere followers of the dogs, as mere *spectators*; their praises, if any are called for, are bestowed on the greyhounds, the hounds, the fox, the hare, or the horses. There is a little rivalship in the riding, or in the behaviour of the horses; but this has so little to do with the *personal merit* of the sportsmen, that it never produces a want of good fellowship in the evening of the day. A shooter who has been *missing* all day, must have an uncommon share of good sense, not to feel mortified while the slaughterers are relating the adventures of that day; and this is what cannot exist in the case of the hunters. Bring me into a room, with a dozen men in it, who have been sporting all day; or, rather let me be in an adjoining room, where I can hear the sound of their voices, without being able to distinguish the words, and I will bet ten to one that I tell whether they be hunters or shooters.

I was once acquainted with a *famous shooter* whose name was WILLIAM EWING. He was a barrister of Philadelphia, but became far more renowned by his gun than by his law cases. We spent scores of days together a shooting, and were extremely well matched, I having excellent dogs and caring little about my reputation as a shot, his dogs being good for nothing, and he caring more about his reputation as a shot than as a lawyer. The fact which I am going to relate respecting this gentleman, ought to be a warning to young men, how they become enamoured of this species of vanity. We had gone about ten miles from our home, to shoot where patridges were said to be very plentiful. We found them so. In the course of a November day, he had, just before dark, shot, and sent to the farm-house, or kept in his bag, *ninety-nine* partridges. He made some few *double shots*, and he might have a *miss* or two, for he sometimes shot when out of my sight, on account of the woods. However, he said that he killed at every shot; and, as he had counted the birds, when we went to dinner at the farm-house and when he cleaned his gun, he, just before sun-set, knew that he had killed *ninety-nine* partridges, every one upon the wing, and a great part of them in woods very thickly set with largish trees. It was a grand achievement; but, unfortunately, he wanted to make it *a hundred*. The sun *was setting*, and, in that country, darkness comes almost at once; it is more like the going out of a candle than that of a fire; and I wanted to be off, as we had a very bad road to go, and as he, being under strict petticoat government, to which he most loyally and dutifully submitted, was compelled to get home that night, taking me with him, the vehicle (horse and gig) being mine. I, therefore, pressed him to come away, and moved on myself towards the house (that of OLD JOHN BROWN, in Bucks county, grandfather of that GENERAL BROWN, who gave some of our whiskered heroes such a rough handling last war, which was waged for the purpose of "DEPOSING JAMES MADISON"), at which house I would have stayed all night, but from which I was compelled to go by that watchful government, under which he had the good fortune to live. Therefore I was in haste to be off. No: he would kill the *hundredth* bird! In vain did I talk of the bad road and its many dangers for want of moon. The poor partridges, which we had scattered about, were *calling* all around us; and, just at this moment, up got one under his feet, in a field in which the wheat was three or four inches high. He shot and *missed*.

"That's it," said he, running as if to *pick up* the bird. "What!" said I, "you don't think you *killed*, do you? Why there is the bird now, not only alive, but *calling*, in that wood"; which was at about a hundred yards distance. He, in that *form of words* usually employed in such cases, asserted that he shot the bird and saw it fall; and I, in much about the same form of words, asserted, that he had *missed*, and that I, with my own eyes, saw the bird fly into the wood. This was too much! To *miss* once out of a hundred times! To lose such a chance of immortality! He was a good-humoured man; I liked him very much; and I could not help feeling for him, when he said, "Well, Sir, I killed the bird; and if you choose to go away and take your dog away, so as to prevent me from *finding* it, you must do it; the dog is *yours*, to be sure." "The *dog*," said I, in a very mild tone, "why, EWING, there is the spot; and could we not see it, upon this smooth green surface, if it were there?" However, he began to *look about*; and I called the dog, and affected to *join him in the search*. Pity for his weakness got the better of my dread of the bad road. After walking backward and forward many times upon about twenty yards square with our eyes to the ground, looking for what both of us knew was not there, I had *passed him* (he going one way and I the other), and I happened to be turning round just after I had passed him; when I saw him, putting his hand behind him, *take a partridge out of his bag and let it fall upon the ground!* I felt no temptation to detect him, but turned away my head, and kept looking about. Presently he, having returned to the spot where the bird was, called out to me, in a most triumphant tone; "*Here! here!* Come here!" I went up to him, and he, pointing with his finger down to the bird, and looking hard in my face at the same time, said, "There, Cobbett; I hope that will be a *warning* to you never to be obstinate again"! "Well," said I, "come along": and away we went as merry as larks. When we got to Brown's, he told them the story, triumphed over me most clamorously; and, though he often repeated the story to my face, I never had the heart to let him know, that I knew of the imposition, which puerile vanity had induced so sensible and honourable a man to be mean enough to practise. A *professed shot* is, almost always, a very disagreeable brother sportsman. He must, in the first place, have a head rather of the emptiest to *pride himself* upon so poor a talent. Then he is always out of temper, if the game fail, or if he miss it. He never participates in that great delight which all sensible men enjoy at beholding the beautiful action, the docility, the zeal, the wonderful sagacity, of the pointer and the setter. He is always thinking about *himself*; always anxious to surpass his companions. I remember that, once, Ewing and I had lost our dog. We were in a wood, and the dog had gone out, and found a covey in a wheat stubble joining the wood. We had been whistling and calling him for, perhaps, half an hour, or more. When we came out of the wood we saw him pointing, with one foot up; and, soon after, he, keeping his foot and body unmoved, gently turned round his head towards the spot where he heard us, as if to bid us come on, and, when he saw that we saw him, turned his head back again. I was so delighted, that I stopped to look with admiration. Ewing, astonished at my want of alacrity, pushed on, shot one of the partridges, and thought no more about the conduct of the dog than if the sagacious creature had had nothing at all to do with the matter.

GEORGE HEAD
1782–1855

George Head was a military administrator who served in the Peninsular War and in Canada. After writing a lively account of his travels, he set out in 1835 on what he called a 'desultory ramble' around England to provide the source for a new book. Published in 1836, *A Home Tour Through the Manufacturing Districts of England* contains detail on industry and trade as well as some light-hearted asides on play and games. The extract here about a sports festival on the beach at Southport is a highlight. Head was impressed by the sense of fun that pervaded the day, particularly when the young men dunked for coins in treacle. He loved the 'good fellowship' of the occasion, and his lively account of a community at play shows us how traditional forms of ribald play survived well into the nineteenth century.

from *A Home Tour Through the Manufacturing Districts of England, in the Summer of 1835*

Since I have undertaken to relate a part of the gaieties into which I entered during the few days of my sojourn at Southport, I must add to the foregoing another rural festival, in the way of races and sports, celebrated on the sands. The ceremonial was duly announced some days before by large placards, printed and distributed, to give it publicity. By these it was set forth, that races would take place between donkies, and the spavined old horses used in the bathing-machines; that men would hop in sacks, trundle wheelbarrows blindfold, chase a pig with a soaped tail; and that boys would climb a greased pole for a gold-laced hat, and dip for pieces of drowned money in a bowl of treacle.

There is no physical or moral act of a man's life that so thoroughly assists his independence for the time being, proves good fellowship with all the world, and exhibits him in an undisguised state of nature, as a sound horse-laugh; and for what possible reason the laws of fashion have prohibited that innocent recreation, I never could imagine,—a prohibition which actually causes the countryman to clap his hand before his mouth, in the presence of his superiors, as if there was harm in giving way to such an honest impulse of nature.

Certainly it is very delightful to see people happy, especially when they know not exactly the reason why, yielding involuntarily to the united sympathies of body and mind, in the form aforesaid; but however I might have been naturally predisposed towards this country tournament, there was one part of the exhibition, calculated, I am sure, to unbend muscles rigid as the bow of Ulysses, and this part was that of dipping for the money in treacle.

In the first place the spot chosen for the occasion, was by nature most happily suited to the purpose on the broad sea-shore, while a projecting ridge of sand-hills afforded a convenient position for the crowd which had assembled, consisting of five or six hundred people, to arrange themselves in clusters, and bask at ease among the little mountains. Besides, it was one of the finest of summer evenings.

A table or dresser having been placed on the sands, a huge wooden bowl containing at least a gallon of treacle, was put upon it. The officiating personage having carefully stirred round and round with a stick, ten silver shillings, within the luscious element, the competitors were summoned by sound of horn to the lists; it being previously understood that the hands of each boy were to be tied behind him, and no means allowed, except the assistance of his teeth, to recover the hidden treasure. On such conditions, every prize so fished up, was to be his by right of salvage.

The first candidate was a great lubberly boy of seventeen, whose diffidence, excited by the gaze of the multitude, caused him to display to better advantage the wide mouth and projecting teeth with which nature had furnished him. Shouts resounded on all sides, and appeals were made from intimate friends to his acquaintanceship, as without delay they proceeded to business. All preparations were effected in a few minutes,—his hands were bound, his throat was bared, he was placed kneeling on the table, the bowl of treacle before him, and he was just ready to duck for the prize, when a desperate effort was made by his grandmother to prevent the ceremony. At this juncture, she very opportunely made her appearance, loudly called him by his name, screamed, pushed the people on her right and on her left, abused both him and them, using her feeble strength to make way through the crowd, and seize her recreant relative. But the poor old creature had very little chance, as might well be supposed, of attaining her object. She was pushed, and hustled, and impeded in all sorts of ways; while on the contrary, the boy was urged and instigated to be undutiful by public acclamation. Recognizing his grandmother (and her solicitude and inflexibility ought certainly to have won his heart,) he grinned clownishly, and as if giving way to a sense of duty, for a moment refrained.—It was but for a moment. The sounds of *"Go it, Dick," "Down with your muzzle,"* were too animating, and urged by the joint love of fame, money and treacle, down went his head into the bowl.

The first struggle was a very determined one; no matter whether or not it was successful, but it may well be asserted, that few scenes of the sort ever presented a better subject for a painter than the one in question, at the moment when, after the first plunge, this rustic renegade drew his head out of the bowl, and recovered his kneeling position. His own countenance more like that of an ourang outang, than anything human, the disappointed rage of the grandmother, and the roars of laughter, proceeding from five or six hundred open mouths in unison, were so many sounds and objects which, when combined, presented, in their way, a picture of real life, seldom if ever to be surpassed.

The festivities lasted upwards of three hours, when even before the sun had set, the country people returned to their homes, and the waves broke again in solitude on the shore. During the whole performance, I never witnessed among a multitude of people, more good-humoured and orderly behaviour; indeed they submitted to be ridden at and driven out of the course by mounted horsemen, with infinitely less remonstrance than is usual with many an ignorant vagabond, who does not reflect that the process is for the general good. In fact the congregation consisted chiefly of sensible industrious people,—of such as, thank God! there are thousands upon thousands in the country, apart from great towns, who support themselves by daily labour, and pass the chief part of their time in the bosoms of their families. In the neighbourhood of Southport, there is a rural manufacturing, as well as agricultural population, of whom these were a part; domestic silk weavers, living separately in small cottages, and working at home at their looms.

CHARLES DICKENS
1812–1870

Novelist Charles Dickens created some of the most memorable stories in Victorian literature, and his characters are wonderfully memorable for their virtues and vices. Samuel Pickwick, the eponymous hero of Dickens's first novel, *The Posthumous Papers of the Pickwick Club*, is one of his most famous. The novel follows the innocent and trusting Pickwick and his friends through their adventures around the country, which include some notable sporting endeavours. They join in a comic cricket match between All-Muggleton and Dingley Dell, and, in this extract, risk the ice for some social skating near Manor Farm. Dickens was always keen to highlight hypocrisy, and Pickwick channels this in calling out Mr Winkle as an 'impostor' for over-hyping his skating ability. The comedy is restored by Pickwick's accident on thin ice, and Pickwick is restored by three bowls of hot punch.

"Now," said Wardle, after a substantial lunch, with the agreeable items of strong-beer and cherry-brandy, had been done ample justice to; "what say you to an hour on the ice? We shall have plenty of time."

"Capital!" said Mr. Benjamin Allen.

"Prime!" ejaculated Mr. Bob Sawyer.

"You skait, of course, Winkle?" said Wardle.

"Ye—yes; oh, yes;" replied Mr. Winkle. "I—I— am *rather* out of practice."

"Oh, *do* skait, Mr. Winkle," said Arabella. "I like to see it so much."

"Oh, it is *so* graceful," said another young lady.

A third young lady said it was elegant, and a fourth expressed her opinion that it was "swan-like."

"I should be very happy, I'm sure," said Mr. Winkle, reddening; "but I have no skaits."

This objection was at once overruled. Trundle had got a couple of pair, and the fat boy announced that there were half-a-dozen more, down stairs, whereat Mr. Winkle expressed exquisite delight, and looked exquisitely uncomfortable.

Old Wardle led the way to a pretty large sheet of ice; and the fat boy and Mr. Weller, having shovelled and swept away the snow which had fallen on it during the night, Mr. Bob Sawyer adjusted his skaits with a dexterity which to Mr. Winkle was perfectly marvellous, and described circles with his left leg, and cut figures of eight; and inscribed upon the ice, without once stopping for breath, a great many other pleasant and astonishing devices, to the excessive satisfaction of Mr. Pickwick, Mr. Tupman, and the ladies; which reached a pitch of positive enthusiasm, when old Wardle and Benjamin Allen, assisted by the aforesaid Bob Sawyer, performed some mystic evolutions, which they called a reel.

All this time, Mr. Winkle, with his face and hands blue with the cold, had been forcing a gimlet into the soles of his feet, and putting his skaits on, with the points behind, and getting the straps into a very complicated and entangled state, with the assistance of Mr. Snodgrass, who knew rather less about skaits than a Hindoo. At length, however, with the assistance of Mr. Weller, the unfortunate skaits were firmly screwed and buckled on, and Mr. Winkle was raised to his feet.

"Now, then, Sir," said Sam, in an encouraging tone; "off vith you, and show 'em how to do it."

"Stop, Sam, stop," said Mr. Winkle, trembling violently, and clutching hold of Sam's arms with the grasp of a drowning man. "How slippery it is, Sam!"

"Not an uncommon thing upon ice, Sir," replied Mr. Weller. "Hold up, Sir."

This last observation of Mr. Weller's bore reference to a demonstration Mr. Winkle made at the instant, of a frantic desire to throw his feet in the air, and dash the back of his head on the ice.

"These—these—are very awkward skaits; ain't they, Sam?" inquired Mr. Winkle, staggering.

"I'm afeerd there's a orkard gen'lm'n in 'em, Sir," replied Sam.

"Now, Winkle," cried Mr. Pickwick, quite unconscious that there was anything the matter. "Come; the ladies are all anxiety."

"Yes, yes," replied Mr. Winkle, with a ghastly smile. "I'm coming."

"Just a goin' to begin," said Sam, endeavouring to disengage himself. "Now, Sir, start off."

"Stop an instant, Sam," gasped Mr. Winkle, clinging most affectionately to Mr. Weller. "I find I've got a couple of coats at home, that I don't want, Sam. You may have them, Sam."

"Thank'ee, Sir," replied Mr. Weller.

"Never mind touching your hat, Sam," said Mr. Winkle, hastily. "You needn't take your hand away, to do that. I meant to have given you five shillings this morning for a Christmas-box, Sam. I'll give it you this afternoon, Sam."

"You're wery good, Sir," replied Mr. Weller.

"Just hold me at first, Sam; will you?" said Mr. Winkle. "There—that's right. I shall soon get in the way of it, Sam. Not too fast, Sam; not too fast."

Mr. Winkle, stooping forward, with his body half doubled up, was being assisted over the ice by Mr. Weller, in a very singular and un-swan-like manner, when Mr. Pickwick most innocently shouted from the opposite bank—

"Sam!"

"Sir?" said Mr. Weller.

"Here. I want you."

"Let go, Sir," said Sam. "Don't you hear the governor a callin'? Let go, Sir."

With a violent effort, Mr. Weller disengaged himself from the grasp of the agonized Pickwickian; and, in so doing, administered a considerable impetus to the unhappy Mr. Winkle. With an accuracy which no degree of dexterity or practice could have insured, that unfortunate gentleman bore swiftly down into the centre of the reel, at the very moment when Mr. Bob Sawyer was performing a flourish of unparalleled beauty. Mr. Winkle struck wildly against him, and with a loud crash they both fell heavily down. Mr. Pickwick ran to the spot. Bob Sawyer had risen to his feet, but Mr. Winkle was far too wise to do anything of the kind in skaits. He was seated on the ice, making spasmodic efforts to smile; but anguish was depicted on every lineament of his countenance.

"Are you hurt?" inquired Mr. Benjamin Allen, with great anxiety.

"Not much," said Mr. Winkle, rubbing his back very hard.

"I wish you'd let me bleed you," said Mr. Benjamin with great eagerness.

"No, thank you," replied Mr. Winkle hurriedly.

"I really think you had better," said Allen.

"Thank you," replied Mr. Winkle; "I'd rather not."

"What do *you* think, Mr. Pickwick?" inquired Bob Sawyer.

Mr. Pickwick was excited and indignant. He beckoned to Mr. Weller, and said in a stern voice, "Take his skaits off."

"No; but really I had scarcely begun," remonstrated Mr. Winkle.

"Take his skaits off," repeated Mr. Pickwick firmly.

The command was not to be resisted. Mr. Winkle allowed Sam to obey it, in silence.

"Lift him up," said Mr. Pickwick. Sam assisted him to rise.

Mr. Pickwick retired a few paces apart from the by-standers; and, beckoning his friend to approach, fixed a searching look upon him, and uttered in a low, but distinct and emphatic tone, these remarkable words:

"You're a humbug, Sir."

"A what!" said Mr. Winkle, starting.

"A humbug, Sir. I will speak plainer, if you wish it. An impostor, Sir."

With these words, Mr. Pickwick turned slowly on his heel, and rejoined his friends.

While Mr. Pickwick was delivering himself of the sentiment just recorded, Mr. Weller and the fat boy, having by their joint endeavours cut out a slide, were exercising themselves thereupon, in a very masterly and brilliant manner. Sam Weller, in particular, was displaying that beautiful feat of fancy sliding which is currently denominated "knocking at the cobbler's door," and which is achieved by skimming over the ice on one foot, and occasionally giving a two-penny postman's knock upon it with the other. It was a good long slide, and there was something in the motion which Mr. Pickwick, who was very cold with standing still, could not help envying.

"It looks a nice warm exercise that, doesn't it?" he enquired of Wardle, when that gentleman was thoroughly out of breath, by reason of the indefatigable manner in which he had converted his legs into a pair of compasses, and drawn complicated problems on the ice.

"Ah, it does, indeed," replied Wardle. "Do you slide?"

"I used to do so, on the gutters, when I was a boy," replied Mr. Pickwick.

"Try it now," said Wardle.

"Oh, do, please Mr. Pickwick," cried all the ladies.

"I should be very happy to afford you any amusement," replied Mr. Pickwick, "but I haven't done such a thing these thirty years."

"Pooh! pooh! nonsense!" said Wardle, dragging off his skaits with the impetuosity which characterised all his proceedings. "Here; I'll keep you company; come along." And away went the good-tempered old fellow down the slide, with a rapidity which came very close upon Mr. Weller, and beat the fat boy all to nothing.

Mr. Pickwick paused, considered, pulled off his gloves and put them in his hat, took two or three short runs, baulked himself as often, and at last took another run and went slowly and gravely down the slide, with his feet about a yard and a quarter apart, amidst the gratified shouts of all the spectators.

"Keep the pot a bilin', Sir," said Sam; and down

went Wardle again, and then Mr. Pickwick, and then Sam, and then Mr. Winkle, and then Mr. Bob Sawyer, and then the fat boy, and then Mr. Snodgrass, following closely upon each other's heels, and running after each other with as much eagerness as if all their future prospects in life depended on their expedition.

It was the most intensely interesting thing, to observe the manner in which Mr. Pickwick performed his share in the ceremony: to watch the torture of anxiety with which he viewed the person behind, gaining upon him at the imminent hazard of tripping him up: to see him gradually expend the painful force which he had put on at first, and turn slowly round on the slide, with his face towards the point from which he had started: to contemplate the playful smile which mantled on his face when he had accomplished the distance, and the eagerness with which he turned round when he had done so, and ran after his predecessor, his black gaiters tripping pleasantly through the snow, and his eyes beaming cheerfulness and gladness through his spectacles. And when he was knocked down, (which happened upon the average every third round), it was the most invigorating sight that can possibly be imagined, to behold him gather up his hat, gloves, and handkerchief, with a glowing countenance, and resume his station in the rank, with an ardour and enthusiasm which nothing could abate.

The sport was at its height, the sliding was at the quickest, the laughter was at the loudest, when a sharp smart crack was heard. There was a quick rush towards the bank, a wild scream from the ladies, and a shout from Mr. Tupman. A large mass of ice disappeared, the water bubbled up over it, and Mr. Pickwick's hat, gloves, and handkerchief were floating on the surface; and this was all of Mr. Pickwick that anybody could see.

Dismay and anguish were depicted on every countenance; the males turned pale, and the females fainted; Mr. Snodgrass and Mr. Winkle grasped each other by the hand, and gazed at the spot where their leader had gone down, with frenzied eagerness; while Mr. Tupman, by way of rendering the promptest assistance, and at the same time conveying to any persons who might be within hearing, the clearest possible notion of the catastrophe, ran off across the country at his utmost speed, screaming "Fire!" with all his might and main.

It was at this very moment, when old Wardle and Sam Weller were approaching the hole with cautious steps, and Mr. Benjamin Allen was holding a hurried consultation with Mr Bob Sawyer, on the advisability of bleeding the company generally, as an improving little bit of professional practice—it was at this very moment that a face, head, and shoulders emerged from beneath the water, and disclosed the features and spectacles of Mr. Pickwick.

"Keep yourself up for an instant—for only one instant," bawled Mr. Snodgrass.

"Yes, do; let me implore you—for my sake," roared Mr. Winkle, deeply affected. The adjuration was rather unnecessary; the probability being, that if Mr. Pickwick had declined to keep himself up for anybody else's sake, it would have occurred to him that he might as well do so, for his own.

"Do you feel the bottom there, old fellow?" said Wardle.

"Yes, certainly," replied Mr. Pickwick, wringing the water from his head and face, and gasping for breath. "I fell upon my back. I couldn't get on my feet at first."

The clay upon so much of Mr. Pickwick's coat as was yet visible, bore testimony to the accuracy of this statement; and as the fears of the spectators were still further relieved by the fat boy's suddenly recollecting that the water was nowhere more than five feet deep, prodigies of valour were performed to get him out. After a vast quantity of splashing, and cracking, and struggling, Mr. Pickwick was at length fairly extricated from his unpleasant position, and once more stood on dry land.

"Oh, he'll catch his death of cold," said Emily.

"Dear old thing!" said Arabella. "Let me wrap this shawl round you, Mr. Pickwick."

"Ah, that's the best thing you can do," said Wardle; "and when you've got it on, run home as fast as your legs can carry you, and jump into bed directly."

A dozen shawls were offered on the instant; and three or four of the thickest having been selected, Mr. Pickwick was wrapped up, and started off, under the guidance of Mr. Weller; presenting the singular phenomenon of an elderly gentleman dripping wet, and without a hat, with his arms bound down to his sides, skimming over the ground without any clearly defined purpose, at the rate of six good English miles an hour.

But Mr. Pickwick cared not for appearances in such an extreme case, and urged on by Sam Weller, he kept at the very top of his speed until he reached the door of Manor Farm, where Mr. Tupman had arrived some five minutes before, and had frightened the old lady into palpitations of the heart, by impressing her with the unalterable conviction that the kitchen chimney was on fire—a calamity which always presented itself in the most glowing colours to the old lady's mind, when anybody about her evinced the smallest agitation.

Mr. Pickwick paused not an instant until he was snug in bed. Sam Weller lighted a blazing fire in the room, and took up his dinner, a bowl of punch was carried up afterwards, and a grand carouse held in honour of his safety. Old Wardle would not hear of his rising, so they made the bed the chair, and Mr. Pickwick presided. A second and a third bowl were ordered in; and when Mr. Pickwick awoke next morning, there was not a symptom of rheumatism about him, which proves, as Mr. Bob Sawyer very justly observed, that there is nothing like hot punch in such cases, and that if ever hot punch did fail to act as a preventive, it was merely because the patient fell into the vulgar error of not taking enough of it.

WILLIAM THACKERAY
1811–1863

William Thackeray's famous novel *Vanity Fair* was published in 1848. It follows the progress of the amoral Rebecca Sharp as she marries and intrigues her way through English society at the time of the Napoleonic Wars. In this extract, we see the country sports of the family's Hampshire estate through the eyes of her neglected eight-year-old son, young Rawdon. The boy idolizes the older men who hunt foxes and set their dogs and ferrets to ratting, though he can only watch excitedly in admiration. Thackeray paints a vivid picture of the brutal masculine sporting domain, where baronets, gentlemen, and the local vicar all join together in displaying their ability to command their dogs and kill wild animals.

from *Vanity Fair*

But Rawdon, as became his age and size, was fonder of the society of the men than of the women; and never wearied of accompanying his sire to the stables, whither the Colonel retired to smoke his cigar—Jim, the Rector's son, sometimes joining his cousin in that and other amusements. He and the Baronet's keeper were very close friends, their mutual taste for "dawgs" bringing them much together. On one day, Mr. James, the Colonel, and Horn, the keeper, went and shot pheasants, taking little Rawdon with them. On another most blissful morning, these four gentlemen partook of the amusement of rat-hunting in a barn, than which sport Rawdon as yet had never seen anything more noble.

They stopped up the ends of certain drains in the barn, into the other openings of which ferrets were inserted; and then stood silently aloof, with uplifted stakes in their hands, and an anxious little terrier (Mr. James's celebrated "dawg" Forceps, indeed,) scarcely breathing from excitement, listening motionless on three legs, to the faint squeaking of the rats below. Desperately bold at last, the persecuted animals bolted above-ground: the terrier accounted for one, the keeper for another; Rawdon, from flurry and excitement, missed his rat, but on the other hand he half-murdered a ferret.

But the greatest day of all was that on which Sir Huddlestone Fuddlestone's hounds met upon the lawn at Queen's Crawley.

That was a famous sight for little Rawdon. At half-past ten, Tom Moody, Sir Huddlestone Fuddlestone's huntsman, was seen trotting up the avenue, followed by the noble pack of hounds in a compact body—the rear being brought up by the two whips clad in stained scarlet frocks—light hard-featured lads on well-bred lean horses, possessing marvellous dexterity in casting the points of their long heavy whips at the thinnest part of any dog's skin who dares to straggle from the main body, or to take the slightest notice, or even so much as wink, at the hares and rabbits starting under their noses.

Next comes boy Jack, Tom Moody's son, who weighs five stone, measures eight-and-forty inches, and will never be any bigger. He is perched on a large raw-boned hunter, half-covered by a capacious saddle. This animal is Sir Huddlestone Fuddlestone's favourite horse—the Nob. Other horses, ridden by other small boys, arrive from time to time, awaiting their masters, who will come cantering on anon.

Tom Moody rides up to the door of the Hall, where he is welcomed by the butler, who offers him drink, which he declines. He and his pack then draw off into a sheltered corner of the lawn, where the dogs roll on the grass, and play or growl angrily at one another, ever and anon breaking out into furious fight speedily to be quelled by Tom's voice, unmatched at rating, or the snaky thongs of the whips.

Many young gentlemen canter up on thoroughbred hacks, spatter-dashed to the knee, and enter the house to drink cherry-brandy and pay their respects to the ladies, or, more modest and sportsman-like, divest themselves of their mud-boots, exchange their hacks for their hunters, and warm their blood by a preliminary gallop round the lawn. Then they collect round the pack in the corner, and talk with Tom Moody of past sport, and the merits of Sniveller and Diamond, and of the state of the country and of the wretched breed of foxes.

Sir Huddlestone presently appears mounted on a clever cob, and rides up to the Hall, where he enters and does the civil thing by the ladies, after which, being a man of few words, he proceeds to business. The hounds are drawn up to the hall-door and little Rawdon descends amongst them, excited yet half alarmed by the caresses which they bestow upon him, at the thumps he receives from their waving tails, and at their canine bickerings, scarcely restrained by Tom Moody's tongue and lash.

Meanwhile, Sir Huddlestone has hoisted himself unwieldily on the Nob: "Let's try Sowster's Spinney, Tom," says the Baronet, "Farmer Mangle tells me there are two foxes in it." Tom blows his horn and trots off, followed by the pack, by the whips, by the young gents from Winchester, by the farmers of the neighborhood, by the labourers of the parish on foot, with whom the day is a great holiday; Sir Huddlestone bringing up the rear with Colonel Crawley, and the whole *cortége* disappears down the avenue.

The Reverend Bute Crawley (who has been too modest to appear at the public meet before his nephew's windows), and whom Tom Moody remembers forty years back a slender divine riding the wildest horses, jumping the widest brooks, and larking over the newest gates in the country,—his Reverence, we say, happens to trot out from the Rectory Lane on his powerful black horse, just as Sir Huddlestone passes; he joins the worthy baronet. Hounds and horsemen disappear, and little Rawdon remains on the door-steps, wondering and happy.

THOMAS HUGHES
1822–1896

Few novelists can be credited with popularizing a
sport and its culture in the way that Thomas Hughes
did for rugby football. Hughes drew on his own
experiences of Rugby School in his novel *Tom
Brown's School Days* of 1857, and helped to establish
the cult of public-school athleticism. The novel follows Tom Brown as he moves from new boy to
adulthood, learning lessons about honour, loyalty,
and how to deal with bullies along the way. The
school's own version of football was central in Tom's
journey, and this immensely popular novel helped to
cement the idea of the playing field as being more
important than the classroom in an English gentleman's education. Here, Tom is introduced to the
game, and goes on to play a heroic role in his first
match. We can sense the intensity of the action,
along with the importance of the traditions and idio-
syncratic language that are an important part of any
sport's culture.

from *Tom Brown's School Days*

But now look, there is a slight move forward of the School-house wings; a shout of "Are you ready?" and loud affirmative reply. Old Brooke takes half-a-dozen quick steps, and away goes the ball spinning towards the School goal,—seventy yards before it touches ground, and at no point above twelve or fifteen feet high, a model kick-off; and the School-house cheer and rush on; the ball is returned, and they meet it and drive it back amongst the masses of the School already in motion. Then the two sides close, and you can see nothing for minutes but a swaying crowd of boys, at one point violently agitated. That is where the ball is, and there are the keen players to be met, and the glory and the hard knocks to be got: you hear the dull thud thud of the ball, and the shouts of, "Off your side," "Down with him," "Put him over," "Bravo." This is what we call a scrummage, gentlemen, and the first scrummage in a School-house match was no joke in the consulship of Plancus.

But see! it has broken; the ball is driven out on the School-house side, and a rush of the School carries it past the School-house players-up. "Look out in quarters," Brooke's and twenty other voices ring out; no need to call though: the School-house captain of quarters has caught it on the bound, dodges the foremost School boys, who are heading the rush, and sends it back with a good drop-kick well into the enemy's country. And then follows rush upon rush, and scrummage upon scrummage, the ball now driven through into the School-house quarters, and now into the School goal; for the School-house have not lost the advantage which the kick-off and a slight wind gave them at the outset, and are slightly "penning" their adversaries. You say, you don't see much in it all; nothing but a struggling mass of boys, and a leather ball which seems to excite them all to great fury, as a red rag does a bull. My dear sir, a battle would look much the same to you, except that the boys would be men, and the balls iron; but a battle would be worth your looking at for all that, and so is a football match. You can't be expected to appreciate the delicate strokes of play, the turns by which a game is lost and won,—it takes an old player to do that, but the broad philosophy of football you can understand if you will. Come along with me a little nearer, and let us consider it together.

The ball has just fallen again where the two sides are thickest, and they close rapidly around it in a scrummage; it must be driven through now by force or skill, till it flies out on one side or the other. Look how differently the boys face it! Here come two of the bulldogs, bursting through the outsiders; in they go, straight to the heart of the scrummage, bent on driving that ball out on the opposite side. That is what they mean to do. My sons, my sons! you are too hot; you have gone past the ball, and must struggle now right through the scrummage, and get round and back again to your own side, before you can be of any further use. Here comes young Brooke; he goes in as straight as you, but keeps his head, and backs and bends, holding himself still behind the ball, and driving it furiously when he gets the chance. Take a leaf out of his book, you young chargers. Here come Speedicut, and Flashman the School-house bully, with shouts and great action. Won't you two come up to young Brooke, after locking-up, by the School-house fire, with "Old fellow, wasn't that just a splendid scrummage by the three trees!" But he knows you, and so do we. You don't really want to drive that ball through that scrummage, chancing all hurt for the glory of the School-house—but to make us think that's what you want—a vastly different thing; and fellows of your kidney will never go through more than the skirts of a scrummage, where it's all push and no kicking. We respect boys who keep out of it, and don't sham going in; but you—we had rather not say what we think of you.

Then the boys who are bending and watching on the outside, mark them—they are most useful players, the dodgers; who seize on the ball the moment it rolls out from amongst the chargers, and away with it across to the opposite goal: they seldom go into the scrummage, but must have more coolness than the chargers: as endless as are boys' characters, so are their ways of facing or not facing a scrummage at football.

Three-quarters of an hour are gone; first winds are failing, and weight and numbers beginning to tell. Yard by yard the School-house have been driven back, contesting every inch of ground. The bull-dogs are the colour of mother earth from shoulder to ankle, except young Brooke, who has a marvellous knack of keeping his legs. The School-house are being penned in their turn, and now the ball is behind their goal, under the Doctor's wall. The Doctor and some of his family are there looking on, and seem as anxious as any boy for the success of the School-house. We get a minute's breathing time before old Brooke kicks out, and he gives the word to play strongly for touch, by the three trees. Away goes the ball, and the bull-dogs after it, and in another minute there is shout of "In touch!" "Our ball!" Now's your time, old Brooke, while your men are still fresh. He stands with the ball in his hand, while the two sides form in deep lines opposite one another: he must strike it straight out between them. The lines are thickest close to him, but young Brooke and two or three of his men are shifting up further, where the opposite line is weak. Old Brooke strikes it out straight and strong, and it falls opposite his brother. Hurra! that rush has taken it right through the School line, and away past the three trees, far into their quarters, and young Brooke and the bull-dogs are close upon it. The School leaders rush back shouting "Look out in goal," and strain every nerve to catch him, but they are after the fleet-est foot in Rugby. There they go straight for the School goal-posts, quarters scattering before them. One after another the bull-dogs go down, but young Brooke holds on. "He is down." No! a long stagger, but the danger is past; that was the shock of Crew, the most dangerous of dodgers. And now he is close to the School goal, the ball not three yards before him. There is a hurried rush of the School fags to the spot, but no one throws himself on the ball, the only chance, and young Brooke has touched it right under the School goal-posts.

The School leaders come up furious, and admin-ister toco to the wretched fags nearest at hand; they may well be angry, for it is all Lombard-street to a china orange that the School-house kick a goal with the ball touched in such a good place. Old Brooke of course will kick it out, but who shall catch and place it? Call Crab Jones. Here he comes, sauntering along with a straw in his mouth, the queerest, coolest fish in Rugby: if he were tumbled into the moon this minute, he would just pick himself up without taking his hands out of his pockets or turning a hair. But it is a moment when the boldest charger's heart beats quick. Old Brooke stands with the ball under his arm motioning the School back; he will not kickout till they are all in goal, behind the posts; they are all edging forwards, inch by inch, to get nearer for the rush at Crab Jones, who stands there in front of old Brooke to catch the ball. If they can reach and destroy him before he catches, the danger is over; and with one and the same rush they will carry it right away to the School-house goal. Fond hope! it is kicked out and caught beautifully. Crab strikes his heel into the ground, to mark the spot where the ball was caught, beyond which the School line may not advance; but there they stand, five deep, ready to rush the moment the ball touches the ground. Take plenty of room! don't give the rush a chance of reaching you! place it true and steady! Trust Crab Jones—he has made a small hole with his heel for the ball to lie on, by which he is resting on one knee, with his eye on old Brooke. "Now!" Crab places the ball at the word, old Brooke kicks, and it rises slowly and truly as the School rush forward.

Then a moment's pause, while both sides look up at the spinning ball. There it flies, straight between the two posts, some five feet above the cross-bar, an unquestioned goal; and a shout of real genuine joy rings out from the School-house players-up, and a faint echo of it comes over the close from the goal-keepers under the Doctor's wall. A goal in the first hour—such a thing hasn't been done in the School-house match these five years.

"Over!" is the cry: the two sides change goals, and the School-house goal-keepers come threading their way across through the masses of the School; the most openly triumphant of them, amongst whom is Tom, a School-house boy of two hours' standing, getting their ears boxed in the transit. Tom indeed is excited beyond measure, and it is all the sixth-form boy, kindest and safest of goal-keepers, has been able to do, to keep him from rushing out whenever the ball has been near their goal. So he holds him by his side, and instructs him in the science of touching.

At this moment Griffith, the itinerant vendor of oranges from Hill Morton, enters the close with his heavy baskets; there is a rush of small boys upon the little pale-faced man, the two sides mingling together, subdued by the great Goddess Thirst, like the English and French by the streams in the Pyrenees. The leaders are past oranges and apples, but some of them visit their coats, and apply innocent-looking ginger-beer bottles to their mouths. It is no ginger-beer though, I fear, and will do you no good. One short mad rush, and then a stitch in the side, and no more honest play; that's what comes of those bottles.

But now Griffith's baskets are empty, the ball is placed again midway, and the School are going to kick off. Their leaders have sent their lumber into goal, and rated the rest soundly, and one hundred and twenty picked players-up are there, bent on retrieving the game. They are to keep the ball in front of the School-house goal, and then to drive it in by sheer strength and weight. They mean heavy play and no mistake, and so old Brooke sees; and places Crab Jones in quarters just before the goal, with four or five picked players, who are to keep the ball away to the sides, where a try at goal, if obtained, will be less dangerous than in front. He himself, and Warner and Hedge, who have saved themselves till now, will lead the charges.

"Are you ready?" "Yes." And away comes the ball kicked high in the air, to give the School time to rush on and catch it as it falls. And here they are amongst us. Meet them like Englishmen, you School-house boys, and charge them home. Now is the time to show what mettle is in you—and there shall be a warm seat by the hall fire, and honour, and lots of bottled beer to-night, for him who does his duty in the next half-hour. And they are well met. Again and again the cloud of their players-up gathers before our goal, and comes threatening on, and Warner or Hedge, with young Brooke and the relics of the bull-dogs, break through and carry the ball back; and old Brooke ranges the field like Job's war-horse: the thickest scrummage parts asunder before his rush, like the waves before a clipper's bows; his cheery voice rings over the field, and his eye is everywhere. And if these miss the ball, and it rolls dangerously in front of our goal, Crab Jones and his men have seized it and sent it away towards the sides with the unerring drop-kick. This is worth living for; the whole sum of school-boy existence gathered up into one straining, struggling half-hour, a half-hour worth a year of common life.

The quarter to five has struck, and the play slackens for a minute before goal; but there is Crew, the artful dodger, driving the ball in behind our goal, on the island side, where our quarters are weakest. Is there no one to meet him? Yes! look at little East! the ball is just at equal distances between the two, and they rush together, the young man of seventeen and the boy of twelve, and kick it at the same moment. Crew passes on without a stagger; East is hurled forward by the shock, and plunges on his shoulder, as if he would bury himself in the ground; but the ball rises straight into the air, and falls behind Crew's back, while the "bravos" of the School-house attest the pluckiest charge of all that hard-fought day. Warner picks East up lame and half stunned, and he hobbles back into goal, conscious of having played the man.

And now the last minutes are come, and the School gather for their last rush, every boy of the hundred and twenty who has a run left in him. Reckless of the defence of their own goal, on they come across the level big-side ground, the ball well down amongst them, straight for our goal, like the column of the Old Guard up the slope at Waterloo. All former charges have been child's play to this. Warner and Hedge have met them, but still on they come. The bull-dogs rush in for the last time; they are hurled over or carried back, striving hand, foot, and eyelids. Old Brooke comes sweeping round the skirts of the play, and turning short round picks out the very heart of the scrummage, and plunges in. It wavers for a moment—he has the ball! No, it has passed him, and his voice rings out clear over the advancing tide, "Look out in goal." Crab Jones catches it for a moment; but before he can kick, the rush is upon him and passes over him; and he picks himself up behind them with his straw in his mouth, a little dirtier, but as cool as ever.

The ball rolls slowly in behind the School-house goal not three yards in front of a dozen of the biggest School players-up.

There stand the School-house praepostor, safest of goal-keepers, and Tom Brown by his side, who has learned his trade by this time. Now is your time, Tom. The blood of all the Browns is up, and the two rush in together, and throw themselves on the ball, under the very feet of the advancing column; the praepostor on his hands and knees arching his back, and Tom all along on his face. Over them topple the leaders of the rush, shooting over the back of the praepostor, but falling flat on Tom, and knocking all the wind out of his small carcase. "Our ball," says the praepostor, rising with his prize; "but get up there, there's a little fellow under you." They are hauled and roll off him, and Tom is discovered a motionless body.

Old Brooke picks him up. "Stand back, give him air," he says; and then feeling his limbs, adds, "No bones broken. How do you feel, young un?"

"Hah-hah," gasps Tom as his wind comes back, "pretty well, thank you—all right."

"Who is he?" says Brooke. "Oh, it's Brown, he's a new boy; I know him," says East, coming up.

"Well, he is a plucky youngster, and will make a player," says Brooke.

And five o'clock strikes. "No side" is called, and the first day of the School-house match is over.

CHARLES DICKENS AND WILKIE COLLINS
1812–1870 and 1824–1889

In 1857, Charles Dickens and his friend the novelist Wilkie Collins undertook a walking tour of Cumberland. They wrote a series of humorous stories about 'The Lazy Tour of Two Idle Apprentices' for the magazines *Household Words* and *Harper's Weekly*. The idleness that the protagonists profess includes an antipathy towards organized sport, which offers a contrast to the positive values that games, particularly in the public schools, were supposed to teach. The hero of one section, Thomas Idle, reflects on his one brush with sport, when he was thrown into a cricket match against his will. Driven by the single principle of avoiding the ball, he makes a mockery of the game and of his friends who take it seriously. The fact that he then credits cricket with giving him a fever, rather than making him healthy, is the final irony. Idle's cynical approach reminds us that some Victorians did not like sport: it was not all about Tom Brown.

from 'The Lazy Tour of Two Idle Apprentices'

While Thomas was lazy, he was a model of health. His first attempt at active exertion and his first suffering from severe illness are connected together by the intimate relations of cause and effect. Shortly after leaving school, he accompanied a party of friends to a cricket-field, in his natural and appropriate character of spectator only. On the ground it was discovered that the players fell short of the required number, and facile Thomas was persuaded to assist in making up the complement. At a certain appointed time, he was roused from peaceful slumber in a dry ditch, and placed before three wickets with a bat in his hand. Opposite to him, behind three more wickets, stood one of his bosom friends, filling the situation (as he was informed) of bowler. No words can describe Mr. Idle's horror and amazement, when he saw this young man—on ordinary occasions, the meekest and mildest of human beings—suddenly contract his eyebrows, compress his lips, assume the aspect of an infuriated savage, run back a few steps, then run forward, and, without the slightest previous provocation, hurl a detestably hard ball with all his might straight at Thomas's legs. Stimulated to preternatural activity of body and sharpness of eye by the instinct of self-preservation,

Mr. Idle contrived, by jumping deftly aside at the right moment, and by using his bat (ridiculously narrow as it was for the purpose) as a shield, to preserve his life and limbs from the dastardly attack that had been made on both, to leave the full force of the deadly missile to strike his wicket instead of his leg; and to end the innings, so far as his side was concerned, by being immediately bowled out. Grateful for his escape he was about to return to the dry ditch, when he was peremptorily stopped, and told that the other side was "going in," and that he was expected to "field." His conception of the whole art and mystery of "fielding," may be summed up in the three words of serious advice which he privately administered to himself on that trying occasion—avoid the ball. Fortified by this sound and salutary principle, he took his own course, impervious alike to ridicule and abuse. Whenever the ball came near him, he thought of his shins, and got out of the way immediately. "Catch it!" "Stop it!" "Pitch it up!" were cries that passed by him like the idle wind that he regarded not. He ducked under it, he jumped over it, he whisked himself away from it on either side. Never once, through the whole innings did he and the ball come together on anything approaching to intimate terms. The unnatural activity of body which was necessarily called forth for the accomplishment of this result threw Thomas Idle, for the first time in his life, into a perspiration. The perspiration, in consequence of his want of practice in the management of that particular result of bodily activity, was suddenly checked; the inevitable chill succeeded; and that, in its turn, was followed by a fever. For the first time since his birth, Mr. Idle found himself confined to his bed for many weeks together, wasted and worn by a long illness, of which his own disastrous muscular exertion had been the sole first cause.

🍂

OUIDA
1839–1908

Ouida was the pen name of the author Maria Louise Ramé, the daughter of an English mother and a French father. She wrote a number of successful serials in magazines in her early twenties, and *Held in Bondage*, published in 1863, was the first novel of her prolific career. The novel, complete with its romantic storylines and its setting amongst army officers, helped to set her reputation as a sensationalist writer. In this extract, the officers visit the Epsom Derby, which by this time had become a premier sporting and social event: indeed, the artist William Frith captured its social scene beautifully in his 1858 painting *Derby Day*. Ouida's description of the hold that the Turf had on men's emotions and wallets confirms the Derby's importance, and the officers' Fortnum and Mason picnic emphasizes their social standing in the huge crowd that the race attracts.

from *Held in Bondage*

The Derby fell late that year. The day was a brilliant, sunshiny one, as it ought to be, for it is the sole day in our existence when we are excited and do not, as usual, think it necessary to be bored to death to save our characters. We confess to a wild anxiety at the magic word 'Start!' to which no other sight on earth could rouse us. We watch with thrilling eagerness the horses rounding the Corner as we should watch the beauty of no Galatea, however irresistible; and we see the favourite do the distance with enthusiastic intoxication, to which all the other excitements on earth could never fire our blood! From my earliest recollection since I rode races with the stable boys at five years old, and was discovered indulging in that reprehensible pastime by my tutor (a mild and inoffensive Ch. Ch. man, to whom 'Bell's Life' was a dead letter, and the chariot-racing at Rome and Elis the only painful reading in the classics), my passion has been the Turf. The Turf!—there must needs be some strange attraction in our English sport. It has lovers more faithful than women ever win; it has victims, voluntary holocausts upon its altars, more numerous than any creed that ever brought men to martyrdom; its iron chains are hugged where other silken fetters have grown wearisome; its fascination lasts, while the taste of the wine may pall and the beauty of feminine grace may satiate. Men are constant to its mystic charms where they tire of love's beguilements; they give with a lavish hand to it what they would deny to any living thing. Olden chivalry, modern ambition, boast no disciples so faithful as the followers of the Turf; and, to the Turf, men yield up what women whom they love would ask in vain; lands, fortunes, years, energies, powers; till their mistress has beggared them of all—even too often robbed them of honour itself!

To the Derby, of course, we went—Curly, I, and some other men, in De Vigne's drag, lunched off Rhenish, and Guinness, and Moët, and all the delicacies Fortnum and Mason ever packed in a hamper for Epsom; and drove back to mess along the crowded road.

LEWIS CARROLL
1832–1898

Lewis Carroll's novel *Alice's Adventures in Wonderland*, published in 1865, remains one of the most popular and influential works of Victorian fiction. Mixing elements of mathematics, logic, nonsense, politics, and satire, Carroll created a unique vision of a world seen through a child's eyes. Carroll's satire extends to sport in the famous croquet match, which Alice has to play to keep the dictatorial Queen amused. With flamingoes for mallets, hedgehogs for balls, and players who play out of turn being threatened with execution, the chaotic game pokes fun at the ever-increasing regulation that so many sports – including, of course, croquet itself – were experiencing at this time. Carroll manages this with a comic touch which has made this impossible match one of the most famous sporting scenes in English literature.

from *Alice's Adventures in Wonderland*

"Get to your places!" shouted the Queen in a voice of thunder, and people began running about in all directions, tumbling up against each other: however, they got settled down in a minute or two, and the game began.

Alice thought she had never seen such a curious croquet-ground in her life: it was all ridges and furrows: the croquet balls were live hedgehogs, and the mallets live flamingoes, and the soldiers had to double themselves up and stand on their hands and feet, to make the arches.

The chief difficulty Alice found at first was in managing her flamingo: she succeeded in getting its body tucked away, comfortably enough, under her arm, with its legs hanging down, but generally, just as she had got its neck nicely straightened out, and was going to give the hedgehog a blow with its head, it *would* twist itself round and look up in her face, with such a puzzled expression that she could not help bursting out laughing; and, when she had got its head down, and was going to begin again, it was very provoking to find that the hedgehog had unrolled itself, and was in the act of crawling away: besides all this, there was generally a ridge or a furrow in the way wherever she wanted to send the hedgehog to, and, as the doubled-up soldiers were always getting up and walking off to other parts of the ground, Alice soon came to the conclusion that it was a very difficult game indeed.

The players all played at once, without waiting for turns, quarrelling all the while, and fighting for the hedgehogs; and in a very short time the Queen was in a furious passion, and went stamping about, and shouting "Off with his head!" or "Off with her head!" about once in a minute.

Alice began to feel very uneasy: to be sure, she had not as yet had any dispute with the Queen, but she knew that it might happen any minute, "and then," thought she, "what would become of me? They're dreadfully fond of beheading people here: the great wonder is, that there's any one left alive!"

She was looking about for some way of escape, and wondering whether she could get away without being seen, when she noticed a curious appearance in the air: it puzzled her very much at first, but after watching it a minute or two she made it out to be a grin, and she said to herself "It's the Cheshire-Cat: now I shall have somebody to talk to."

"How are you getting on?" said the Cat, as soon as there was mouth enough for it to speak with.

Alice waited till the eyes appeared, and then nodded. "It's no use speaking to it," she thought, "till its ears have come, or at least one of them." In another minute the whole head appeared, and then Alice put down her flamingo, and began an account of the game, feeling very glad she had some one to listen to her. The Cat seemed to think that there was enough of it now in sight, and no more of it appeared.

"I don't think they play at all fairly," Alice began, in rather a complaining tone, "and they all quarrel so dreadfully one can't hear oneself speak—and they don't seem to have any rules in particular: at least, if there are, nobody attends to them—and you've no idea how confusing it is all the things being alive: for instance, there's the arch I've got to go through next walking about at the other end of the ground—and I should have croqueted the Queen's hedgehog just now, only it ran away when it saw mine coming!"

"How do you like the Queen?" said the Cat in a low voice.

"Not at all," said Alice: "she's so extremely—" Just then she noticed that the Queen was close behind her, listening: so she went on "—likely to win, that it's hardly worth while finishing the game."

The Queen smiled and passed on.

"Who *are* you talking to?" said the King, coming up to Alice, and looking at the Cat's head with great curiosity.

"It's a friend of mine—a Cheshire-Cat," said Alice: "allow me to introduce it."

"I don't like the look of it at all," said the King: "however, it may kiss my hand, if it likes."

"I'd rather not," the Cat remarked.

"Don't be impertinent," said the King, "and don't look at me like that!" He got behind Alice as he spoke.

"A cat may look at a king," said Alice. "I've read that in some book, but I don't remember where."

"Well, it must be removed," said the King very decidedly; and he called to the Queen, who was passing at the moment, "My dear! I wish you would have this cat removed!"

The Queen had only one way of settling all difficulties, great or small. "Off with his head!" she said without even looking round.

"I'll fetch the executioner myself," said the King eagerly, and he hurried off.

Alice thought she might as well go back and see how the game was going on, as she heard the Queen's voice in the distance, screaming with passion. She had already heard her sentence three of the players to be executed for having missed their turns, and she did not like the look of things at all, as the game was in such confusion that she never knew whether it was her turn or not. So she went off in search of her hedgehog.

The hedgehog was engaged in a fight with another hedgehog, which seemed to Alice an excellent opportunity for croqueting one of them with the other: the only difficulty was, that her flamingo was gone across to the other side of the garden, where Alice could see it trying in a helpless sort of way to fly up into a tree.

By the time she had caught the flamingo and brought it back, the fight was over, and both the hedgehogs were out of sight: "but it doesn't matter much," thought Alice, "as all the arches are gone from this side of the ground." So she tucked it away under her arm, that it might not escape again, and went back to have a little more conversation with her friend.

GEORGE GISSING
1857–1903

Novelist George Gissing was most famous for his
stories of urban working-class life, but he also wrote
about wealthier families, and in his early novel *Isabel
Clarendon* of 1885 he set some of the action in the
country houses of the rich. In this extract, we catch
a glimpse of the place that sport and physical culture
had in the lives of the sons of this class. The four
Stratton boys – two in military training and two still
at school – spend their time indoors in boxing,
single-stick, weightlifting, and gymnastics, while
outdoors they hunt or get in fights with local boys.
Gissing gently satirizes their brutal pursuits, particularly when noting that their mother would think they
were ill if they were not so 'riotous', and she clearly
values brawn over brains.

from *Isabel Clarendon*

Mrs. Stratton was summoned home by her husband's arrival just before Christmas. Isabel preferred to delay yet a little, and reached Chislehurst a fortnight later, accomplishing the journey with the assistance of her maid only. It proved rather too much for her strength, and for a day or two she had to keep her room. Then she joined the family, very pale still, and not able to do much more than hold a kind of court throned by the fireside, but with the light of happiness on her face, listening with a bright smile to every one's conversation, equally interested in Master Edgar's latest exploit by flood or field, and in his mother's rather trenchant comments on neighbouring families.

All the Strattons were at home. The four British youths had been keeping what may best be described by Coleridge's phrase, "Devil's Yule." Colonel Stratton was by good luck a man of substance, and could maintain an establishment corresponding to the needs of such a household. Though Mrs. Stratton had spoken of her house as being too large, it would scarcely be deemed so by the guests of mature age who shared it with the two young Strattons already at Woolwich and Sandhurst, and the other two who were still mewing their mighty youth at scholastic institutions. There was a certain upper chamber in which were to be found appliances for the various kinds of recreation sought after by robust young Britons; here they put on "gloves," and pummelled each other to their hearts' satisfaction—thud—thud! Here they vied with one another at single-stick—thwack—thwack! Here they swung dumb-bells, and tumbled on improvised trapezes. And hence, when their noble minds yearned for variety, they rushed headlong, pell-mell into the lower regions of the house, to the delights of the billiard-room. They had the use of a couple of horses, and the frenzy of their over-full veins drove them in turns, like demon huntsmen, over the frozen or muddy country. They returned at the hour of dinner, and ate—ate in stolid silence, till they had appeased the gnawing of hunger, then flung themselves here and there about the drawing-room till their thoughts, released from the brief employment of digestion, could formulate remarks on such subjects as interest youth of their species.

Mrs. Stratton enjoyed it all. Her offspring were perfect in her eyes. Had they been less riotous she would have conceived anxiety about their health. When her third boy, Reginald, aged thirteen years, fell to fisticuffs with a youthful tramp in a lane hard by, and came home irrecognisable from blood and dirt, she viewed him with amused astonishment, and, after setting him to rights with sponge and sticking-plaster, laughingly recommended that in future he should fight only with his social equals. With the two eldest she was a sort of sister; they walked with her about the garden with their arms over her shoulders; the confidence between her and them was perfect, and certainly they were very fond of her. They were stalwart young ruffians, these two, with immaculate complexions and the smooth roundness of feature which entitles men to be called handsome by ladies who are addicted to the use of that word. Mrs. Stratton would rather have been their mother than have borne Shakespeare and Michael Angelo as twins.

JEROME K. JEROME
1859–1927

Over a century after its first appearance in 1889, Jerome K. Jerome's *Three Men in a Boat* remains a well-loved take on the leisurely life of the Victorian middle classes. The plot is simple: the narrator J, and his friends George and Harris, all employed in sedentary occupations, decide they need a holiday. They plump for a two-week boat trip along the Thames from Kingston to Oxford. Jerome planned the book as a travelogue, but his ability to make humour out of any situation quickly turned into a comic novel. The boating holiday, full of mishaps and misadventures as well as rest and relaxation for the trio, is a classic Victorian meeting point of sport and leisure. Boats, like the bicycles in H. G. Wells's writings, can be used for competition and play in the Victorian sporting boom. In this extract, the hapless pleasure sailors crash into a party of anglers, a messy meeting of old and new sportsmen on the water.

from *Three Men in a Boat*

We went through Maidenhead quickly, and then eased up, and took leisurely that grand reach beyond Boulter's and Cookham locks. Clieveden Woods still wore their dainty dress of spring, and rose up, from the water's edge, in one long harmony of blended shades of fairy green. In its unbroken loveliness this is, perhaps, the sweetest stretch of all the river, and lingeringly we slowly drew our little boat away from its deep peace.

We pulled up in the backwater, just below Cookham, and had tea; and, when we were through the lock, it was evening. A stiffish breeze had sprung up—in our favour, for a wonder; for, as a rule on the river, the wind is always dead against you whatever way you go. It is against you in the morning, when you start for a day's trip, and you pull a long distance, thinking how easy it will be to come back with the sail. Then, after tea, the wind veers round, and you have to pull hard in its teeth all the way home.

When you forget to take the sail at all, then the wind is consistently in your favour both ways. But there! This world is only a probation, and man was born to trouble as the sparks fly upward.

This evening, however, they had evidently made a mistake, and had put the wind round at our back instead of in our face. We kept very quiet about it, and got the sail up quickly before they found it out, and then we spread ourselves about the boat in thoughtful attitudes, and the sail bellied out, and strained, and grumbled at the mast, and the boat flew.

I steered.

There is no more thrilling sensation I know of than sailing. It comes as near to flying as man has got to yet—except in dreams. The wings of the rushing wind seem to be bearing you onward, you know not where. You are no longer the slow, plodding, puny thing of clay, creeping tortuously upon the ground; you are a part of Nature! Your heart is throbbing against hers! Her glorious arms are round you, raising you up against her heart! Your spirit is at one with hers; your limbs grow light! The voices of the air are singing to you. The earth seems far away and little; and the clouds, so close above your head, are brothers, and you stretch your arms to them.

We had the river to ourselves, except that, far in the distance, we could see a fishing-punt, moored in mid-stream, on which three fishermen sat; and we skimmed over the water, and passed the wooded banks, and no one spoke.

I was steering.

As we drew nearer, we could see that the three men fishing seemed old and solemn-looking men. They sat on three chairs in the punt, and watched intently their lines. And the red sunset threw a mystic light upon the waters, and tinged with fire the towering woods, and made a golden glory of the piled-up clouds. It was an hour of deep enchantment, of ecstatic hope and longing. The little sail stood out against the purple sky, the gloaming lay around us, wrapping the world in rainbow shadows; and, behind us, crept the night.

We seemed like knights of some old legend, sailing across some mystic lake into the unknown realm of twilight, unto the great land of the sunset.

We did not go into the realm of twilight; we went slap into that punt, where those three old men were fishing. We did not know what had happened at first, because the sail shut out the view, but from the nature of the language that rose up upon the evening air, we gathered that we had come into the neighbourhood of human beings, and that they were vexed and discontented.

Harris let the sail down, and then we saw what had happened. We had knocked those three old gentlemen off their chairs into a general heap at the bottom of the boat, and they were now slowly and painfully sorting themselves out from each other, and picking fish off themselves; and as they worked, they cursed us—not with a common cursory curse, but with long, carefully-thought-out, comprehensive curses, that embraced the whole of our career, and went away into the distant future, and included all our relations, and covered everything connected with us—good, substantial curses.

Harris told them they ought to be grateful for a little excitement, sitting there fishing all day, and he also said that he was shocked and grieved to hear men their age give way to temper so.

But it did not do any good.

George said he would steer, after that. He said a mind like mine ought not to be expected to give itself away in steering boats—better let a mere common-place human being see after that boat, before we jolly well all got drowned; and he took the lines, and brought us up to Marlow.

And at Marlow we left the boat by the bridge, and went and put up for the night at the "Crown."

GEORGE MOORE
1852–1933

The Derby was a highlight of the Victorian calendar, bringing people of all classes together for a day of horse-racing and a funfair atmosphere on Epsom Downs. In this extract from his realist novel *Esther Waters* of 1894, which is set in the 1870s, Irish novelist George Moore shows us the switchback, the model horses on which punters can emulate the professional jockeys, the sideshows, the coconut shies and more, all through the gaze of Esther, a young working-class woman who is dazzled by the glamour of the day. As with so many other sporting events, the excitement of the occasion provides the scene for flirtation, all played out in one of the biggest spectator events of its time. The horse race itself is almost a footnote to the fair.

The crowd shouted. She looked where the others looked, but saw only the burning blue with the white stand marked upon it. It was crowded like the deck of a sinking vessel, and Esther wondered at the excitement, the cause of which was hidden from her. She wandered to the edge of the crowd until she came to a chalk road where horses and mules were tethered. A little higher up she entered the crowd again, and came suddenly upon a switchback railway. Full of laughing and screaming girls it bumped over a middle hill, and then rose slowly till it reached the last summit. It was shot back again into the midst of its fictitious perils, and this mock voyaging was accomplished to the sound of music from a puppet orchestra. Bells and drums, a life and a triangle, cymbals clashed mechanically, and a little soldier beat the time. Further on, under a striped awning, were the wooden horses. They were arranged so well that they rocked to and fro, imitating as nearly as possible the action of real horses. Esther watched the riders. A blue skirt looked like a riding habit, and a girl in a salmon pink leaned back in her saddle just as if she had been taught how to ride. A girl in a grey jacket encouraged a girl in white who rode a grey horse. But before Esther could make out for certain that the man in the blue Melton jacket was Bill Evans he had passed out of sight, and she had to wait until his horse came round the second time. At that moment she caught sight of the red poppies in Sarah's hat.

The horses began to slacken speed. They went slower and slower, then stopped altogether. The riders began to dismount and Esther pressed through the bystanders, fearing she would not be able to overtake her friends.

"Oh, here you are," said Sarah. "I thought I never should find you again. How hot it is!"

"Were you on in that ride? Let's have another, all three of us. These three horses."

Round and round they went, their steeds bobbing nobly up and down to the sound of fifes, drums and cymbals. They passed the winning-post many times; they had to pass it five times, and the horse that stopped nearest it won the prize. A long drawn-out murmur continuous as the sea, swelled up from the course, a murmur, which at last passed into words: "Here they come; blue wins, the favourite's beat." Esther paid little attention to these cries; she did not understand them, they reached her indistinctly, and soon died away, absorbed in the strident music that accompanied the circling horses. These had now begun to slacken speed ... They went slower and slower. Sarah and Bill, who rode side by side, seemed like winning, but at the last moment they glided by the winning-post. Esther's steed stopped in time, and she was told to choose a china mug from a great heap.

"You've all the luck to-day," said Bill. "Hayfield, who was backed all the winter, broke down a month ago . . . 2 to 1 against Fly-leaf, 4 to 1 against Signet-Ring, 4 to 1 against Dewberry, 10 to 1 against Vanguard, the winner at 50 to 1 offered. Your husband must have won a little fortune. Never was there such a day for the bookies."

Esther said she was very glad, and was undecided which mug she should choose. At last she saw one on which "Jack" was written in gold letters. They then visited the peep-shows, and especially liked St. James' Park with the Horse Guards out on parade; the Spanish bull-fight did not stir them, and Sarah couldn't find a single young man to her taste in the House of Commons. Among the performing birds they liked best a canary that climbed a ladder. Bill was attracted by the American strength-testers, and he gave an exhibition of his muscle to Sarah's very great admiration. They all had some shies at cocoa-nuts, and passed by J. Bilton's great bowling saloon without visiting it. Once more the air was rent with cries of "Here they come! Here they come!" Even the 'commodation men left their canvas shelters and pressed forward inquiring which had won. A moment after a score of pigeons floated and flew through the blue air and then departed in different directions, some making straight for London, others for the blue mysterious evening that had risen about the Downs—the sun-baked Downs strewed with waste paper and covered with tipsy men and women,—a screaming and disordered animality.

"Well, so you've come back at last," said William. "The favourite was beaten. I suppose you know that a rank outsider won. But what about this gentleman?"

"Met these 'ere ladies on the 'ill an' been showing them over the course. No offence, I hope, guv'nor?"

William did not answer, and Bill took leave of Sarah in a manner that told Esther that they had arranged to meet again.

"Where did you pick up that bloke?"

"He came up and spoke to us, and Esther stopped to speak to the parson."

"To the parson. What do you mean?"

The circumstance was explained, and William asked them what they thought of the racing.

"We didn't see no racing," said Sarah; "we was

on the 'ill on the wooden 'orses. Esther's 'orse won. She got a mug; show the mug, Esther."

"So you saw no Derby after all?" said William.

"Saw no racin'," said his neighbour; "ain't she won the cup?"

The joke was lost on the women, who only perceived that they were being laughed at.

"Come up here, Esther," said William; "stand on my box. The 'orses are just going up the course for the preliminary canter,—and you, Sarah, take Teddy's place. Teddy, get down, and let the lady up."

"Yes, guv'nor. Come up 'ere, ma'am."

"And is those the 'orses?" said Sarah. "They do seem small."

The ringmen roared. "Not up to those on the 'ill, ma'am," said one. "Not such beautiful goers," said another.

There were two or three false starts, and then looking through a multitude of hats Esther saw five or six thin greyhound-looking horses. They passed like shadows, flitted by; and she was sorry for the poor chestnut that trotted in among the crowd.

This was the last race. Once more the favourite had been beaten; there were no bets to pay, and the book-makers began to prepare for departure.

A. E. HOUSMAN
1859–1936

A Shropshire Lad is A. E. Housman's cycle of poems, published in 1896. The poems are suffused with a sense of nostalgia and melancholy for the 'land of lost content' of Housman's childhood, albeit a fictionalized one as he did not grow up in Shropshire. Many of the poems deal with the high ideals and less lofty realities of childhood, and sport figures in two of them. In this sad piece, 'To An Athlete Dying Young', Housman tells of a runner who has earned glory for himself and his town by winning a race, but who has then died – we are not told how. He compares the crowd lifting him aloft after his victory with the pall-bearers carrying his coffin at his funeral. The message is bleak: it is better for this 'smart lad' to die young, in the prime of life, with the trophies still his, than to let age wither him. The book was very popular with soldiers in the First World War: the theme of early death and glorious memories must have resonated with a generation.

'To an Athlete Dying Young' from
A Shropshire Lad

The time you won your town the race
We chaired you through the market-place;
Man and boy stood cheering by,
And home we brought you shoulder-high.

To-day, the road all runners come,
Shoulder-high we bring you home,
And set you at your threshold down,
Townsman of a stiller town.

Smart lad, to slip betimes away
From fields where glory does not stay
And early though the laurel grows
It withers quicker than the rose.

Eyes the shady night has shut
Cannot see the record cut,
And silence sounds no worse than cheers
After earth has stopped the ears:

Now you will not swell the rout
Of lads that wore their honours out,
Runners whom renown outran
And the name died before the man.

So set, before its echoes fade,
The fleet foot on the sill of shade,
And hold to the low lintel up
The still-defended challenge-cup.

And round that early-laurelled head
Will flock to gaze the strengthless dead,
And find unwithered on its curls
The garland briefer than a girl's.

H. G. WELLS
1866–1946

H. G. Wells was one of the most prolific authors of his age, with novels, history books, and political writings to his name. He is best remembered now for his visionary science fiction stories, but his comic stories about ordinary people living modest lives, such as *Kipps* and *The History of Mr Polly*, were also very popular. His 1895 cycling novel *The Wheels of Chance* was within this tradition. It tells the story of a drapery shop worker, Mr Hoopdriver, who escapes his drudgery for a spell by buying a bicycle and taking to the road for a holiday. This extract charts the start of his journey from suburban Putney as he heads to Surrey, Hampshire, and Dorset. Like Jerome's boating novel, it reminds us of the close links between sport and recreation, and it captures the 'Freedom and Adventure' that the mass-produced bicycle brought for the lower-middle classes in Victorian Britain.

from *The Wheels of Chance*

Only those who toil six long days out of the seven, and all the year round, save for one brief glorious fortnight or ten days in the summer time, know the exquisite sensations of the First Holiday Morning. All the dreary, uninteresting routine drops from you suddenly, your chains fall about your feet. All at once you are Lord of yourself, Lord of every hour in the long, vacant day; you may go where you please, call none Sir or Madam, have a lappel free of pins, doff your black morning coat and wear the colour of your heart, and be a Man. You grudge sleep, you grudge eating and drinking even, their intrusion on those exquisite moments. There will be no more rising before breakfast in casual old clothing, to go dusting and getting ready in a cheerless, shutter-darkened, wrappered-up shop; no more imperious cries of, "Forward, Hoopdriver," no more hasty meals, and weary attendance on fitful old women, for ten blessed days. The first morning is by far the most glorious, for you hold your whole fortune in your hands. Thereafter, every night, comes a pang, a spectre, that will not be exorcised—the premonition of the return. The shadow of going back, of being put in the cage again for another twelve months, lies blacker and blacker across the sunlight. But on the first morning of the ten the holiday has no past, and ten days seems as good as infinity.

And it was fine, full of a promise of glorious days, a deep blue sky, with dazzling piles of white cloud here and there, as though celestial haymakers had been piling the swathes of last night's clouds into cocks for a coming cartage. There were thrushes in the Richmond Road, and a lark on Putney Heath. The freshness of dew was in the air; dew or the relics of an overnight shower glittered on the leaves and grass. Hoopdriver had breakfasted early by Mrs. Gunn's complaisance. He wheeled his machine up Putney Hill, and his heart sang within him. Half-way up, a dissipated-looking black cat rushed home across the road and vanished under a gate. All the big red-brick houses behind the variegated shrubs and trees had their blinds down still, and he would not have changed places with a soul in any one of them for a hundred pounds.

He had on his new brown cycling suit—a handsome Norfolk jacket thing for 30s.—and his legs—those martyr legs—were more than consoled by thick chequered stockings, "thin in the foot, thick in the leg," for all they had endured. A neat packet of American cloth behind the saddle contained his change of raiment, and the bell, and the handle-bar, and the hubs and lamp, albeit a trifle freckled by wear, glittered blindingly in the rising sunlight. And at the top of the hill, after only one unsuccessful attempt, which, somehow, terminated on the green, Hoopdriver mounted, and, with a stately and cautious restraint in his pace, and a dignified curvature of path, began his great Cycling Tour along the Southern Coast.

There is only one phrase to describe his course at this stage, and that is—voluptuous curves. He did not ride fast, he did not ride straight, an exacting critic might say he did not ride well—but he rode generously, opulently, using the whole road and even nibbling at the footpath. The excitement never flagged. So far he had never passed or been passed by anything, but as yet the day was young and the road was clear. He doubted his steering so much that, for the present, he had resolved to dismount at the approach of anything else upon wheels. The shadows of the trees lay very long and blue across the road; the morning sunlight was like amber fire. At the cross-roads at the top of West Hill, where the cattle trough stands, he turned towards Kingston and set himself to scale the little bit of ascent. An early heath-keeper, in his velveteen jacket, marvelled at his efforts; and while he yet struggled the head of a carter rose over the brow.

At the sight of him Mr. Hoopdriver, according to his previous determination, resolved to dismount. He tightened the brake, and the machine stopped dead. He was trying to think what he did with his right leg whilst getting off. He gripped the handles and released the brake, standing on the left pedal and waving his right foot in the air. Then—these things take so long in the telling—he found the machine was falling over to the right. While he was deciding upon a plan of action, gravitation appears to have been busy. He was still irresolute when he found the machine on the ground, himself kneeling upon it, and a vague feeling in his mind that again Providence had dealt harshly with his shin. This happened when he was just level with the heath-keeper. The man in the approaching cart stood up to see the ruins better.

"*That* ain't the way to get off," said the heath-keeper.

Mr. Hoopdriver picked up the machine. The handle was twisted askew again. He said something under his breath. He would have to unscrew the beastly thing.

"*That* ain't the way to get off," repeated the heath-keeper, after a silence.

"*I* know that," said Mr. Hoopdriver testily, determined to overlook the new specimen on his shin at any cost. He unbuckled the wallet behind the saddle, to get out a screw-hammer.

"If you know it ain't the way to get off—whaddyer do it for?" said the heath-keeper, in a tone of friendly controversy.

Mr. Hoopdriver got out his screw-hammer and went to the handle. He was annoyed. "That's my business, I suppose," he said, fumbling with the screw. The unusual exertion had made his hands shake frightfully.

The heath-keeper became meditative, and twisted his stick in his hands behind his back. "You've broken yer 'andle, ain't yer?" he said presently. Just then the screw-hammer slipped off the nut. Mr. Hoopdriver used a nasty, low word.

"They're trying things, them bicycles," said the heath-keeper charitably. "Very trying." Mr. Hoopdriver gave the nut a vicious turn, and suddenly stood up—he was holding the front wheel between his knees. "I wish," said he, with a catch in his voice, "I wish you'd leave off staring at me." Then with the air of one who has delivered an ultimatum, he began replacing the screw-hammer in the wallet.

The heath-keeper never moved. Possibly he raised his eyebrows, and certainly he stared harder than he did before. "You're pretty unsociable," he said slowly, as Mr. Hoopdriver seized the handles and stood ready to mount as soon as the cart had passed.

The indignation gathered slowly but surely. "Why don't you ride on a private road of your own if no one ain't to speak to you?" asked the heath-keeper, perceiving more and more clearly the bearing of the matter. "Can't no one make a passin' remark to you, Touchy? Ain't I good enough to speak to you? Been struck wooden all of a sudden?"

Mr. Hoopdriver stared into the Immensity of the Future. He was rigid with emotion. It was like abusing the Lions in Trafalgar Square. But the heath-keeper felt his honour was at stake.

"Don't you make no remarks to '*im*," said the keeper as the carter came up broadside to them. "'E's a bloomin' dook, 'e is. 'E don't converse with no one under a earl. 'E's off to Windsor, 'e is; that's why 'e's stickin' his be'ind out so haughty. Pride! Why, 'e's got so much of it, 'e has to carry some of it in that there bundle there, for fear 'e'd bust if 'e didn't ease hisself a bit—'*E*——"

But Mr. Hoopdriver heard no more. He was hopping vigorously along the road, in a spasmodic attempt to remount. He missed the treadle once, and swore viciously, to the keeper's immense delight. "Nar! Nar!" said the heath-keeper.

In another moment Mr. Hoopdriver was up, and after one terrific lurch of the machine, the heath-keeper dropped out of earshot.

Mr. Hoopdriver would have liked to look back at his enemy, but he usually twisted round and upset if he tried that. He had to imagine the indignant heath-keeper telling the carter all about it. He tried to infuse as much disdain as possible into his retreating aspect.

He drove on his sinuous way down the dip by the new mere and up the little rise to the crest of the hill that drops into Kingston Vale; and so remarkable is the psychology of cycling, that he rode all the straighter and easier because the emotions the heath-keeper had aroused relieved his mind of the constant expectation of collapse that had previously unnerved him. To ride a bicycle properly is very like a love affair; chiefly it is a matter of faith. Believe you do it, and the thing is done; doubt, and, for the life of you, you cannot.

Now you may perhaps imagine that as he rode on, his feelings towards the heath-keeper were either vindictive or remorseful—vindictive for the aggravation or remorseful for his own injudicious display of ill-temper. As a matter of fact, they were nothing of the sort. A sudden, a wonderful gratitude, possessed him. The Glory of the Holidays had resumed its sway with a sudden accession of splendour. At the crest of the hill he put his feet upon the foot-rests, and now riding moderately straight, went, with a palpitating brake, down that excellent descent. A new delight was in his eyes, quite over and above the pleasure of rushing through the keen, sweet, morning air. He reached out his thumb and twanged his bell out of sheer happiness.

"'He's a bloomin' dook—he is!'" said Mr. Hoopdriver to himself, in a soft undertone, as he went soaring down the hill, and again, "'He's a bloomin' dook!'" He opened his mouth in a silent laugh. It was having a decent cut did it. His social superiority had been so evident that even a man like that noticed it. No more Manchester Department for ten days! Out of Manchester, a Man. The draper Hoopdriver, the Hand, had vanished from existence. Instead was a gentleman, a man of pleasure, with a five-pound note, two sovereigns, and some silver at various convenient points of his person. At any rate as good as a dook, if not precisely in the peerage. Involuntarily at the thought of his funds Hoopdriver's right hand left the handle and sought his breast pocket, to be immediately recalled by a violent swoop of the machine towards the cemetery. Whirroo! Just missed that half-brick! Mischievous brutes there were in the world to put such a thing in the road. Some blooming 'Arry or other! Ought to prosecute a few of these roughs, and the rest would know better. That must be the buckle of the wallet was rattling on the mud-guard. How cheerfully the wheels buzzed!

The cemetery was very silent and peaceful, but the Vale was waking, and windows rattled and squeaked up, and a white dog came out of one of the houses and yelped at him. He got off, rather breathless, at the foot of Kingston Hill, and pushed up. Halfway up, an early milk chariot rattled by him; two dirty men with bundles came hurrying down. Hoopdriver felt sure they were burglars, carrying home the swag.

It was up Kingston Hill that he first noticed a peculiar feeling, a slight tightness at his knees; but he noticed, too, at the top that he rode straighter than he did before. The pleasure of riding straight blotted out these first intimations of fatigue. A man on horseback appeared; Hoopdriver, in a tumult of soul at his own temerity, passed him; then down the hill into Kingston, with the screw-hammer, behind in the wallet, rattling against the oil-can. He passed, without misadventure, a fruiterer's van and a sluggish cartload of bricks. And in Kingston, Hoopdriver, with the most exquisite sensations, saw the shutters half removed from a draper's shop, and two yawning youths, in dusty old black jackets and with dirty white comforters about their necks, clearing up the planks and boxes and wrappers in the window, preparatory to dressing it out. Even so had Hoop-driver been on the previous day. But now, was he not a bloomin' dook, palpably in the sight of common men? Then round the corner to the right—bell banged furiously—and so along the road to Surbiton.

Whoop for Freedom and Adventure! Every now and then a house with an expression of sleepy surprise would open its eye as he passed, and to the right of him for a mile or so the weltering Thames flashed and glittered. Talk of your *joie de vivre*! Albeit with a certain cramping sensation about the knees and calves slowly forcing itself upon his attention.

HENRY NEWBOLT
1862–1938

Poet Henry Newbolt drew on his schooldays at Clifton College, Bristol, in his most famous poem, 'Vitaï Lampada' ('the torch of life') of 1892. The poem epitomizes the links between school, sport, and military service that was such a prevalent ideal in Victorian Britain, with its story of the soldier in an imperial war looking back to the cricket matches of his schooldays for inspiration. The Close of Clifton College is replaced by a desert battlefield, and the opponents are now armed with weapons rather than a cricket ball, but the famous refrain of 'Play up! play up! and play the game' links the two moments. This linkage of sport with imperial service was a cliché even in the 1890s, but it was widespread, and the government's use of sporting images in recruitment materials for the Boer War and the First World War suggests that it resonated deeply in the popular imagination.

'Vitaï Lampada'

There's a breathless hush in the Close to-night—
    Ten to make and the match to win—
A bumping pitch and a blinding light,
    An hour to play and the last man in.
And it's not for the sake of a ribboned coat,
    Or the selfish hope of a season's fame,
But his Captain's hand on his shoulder smote
    "Play up! play up! and play the game!"

The sand of the desert is sodden red,—
    Red with the wreck of a square that broke ;—
The Gatling's jammed and the colonel dead
    And the regiment blind with dust and smoke.
The river of death has brimmed his banks,
    And England's far, and Honour a name,
But the voice of a schoolboy rallies the ranks,
    "Play up! play up! and play the game!"

This is the word that year by year
		While in her place the School is set
Every one of her sons must hear,
		And none that hears it dare forget.
This they all with a joyful mind
		Bear through life like a torch in flame,
And falling fling to the host behind—
		"Play up! play up! and play the game!"

Francis Thompson
1859–1907

Poet and mystic Francis Thompson lived a troubled life, characterized by failed medical studies, ill health, homelessness, and opium addiction. He found some stability under the care of a Roman Catholic community, and published a series of poems inspired by his faith and his visions, most famously in 'The Hound of Heaven'. It might seem incongruous to find him also writing on sport, but Thompson had a lifelong love of cricket, and this comes out in his poem 'At Lord's', written late in his life. It was apparently inspired by a friend inviting him to watch a match at Lord's cricket ground in London. He declines to go, preferring to reminisce on a match between his native Lancashire and Gloucestershire from 1878. In his memory, Lancashire's A. N. Hornby and Dick Barlow and the visitors' famous W. G. Grace stand out. But in the present, he can see only 'shades' and a 'ghostly batsman' as he knows that he is close to death. This is frequently quoted in cricketing literature, and is probably the sport's most famous poem, a perfect combination of excitement, melancholy, and nostalgia.

'At Lord's'

It is little I repair to the matches of the Southron folk,
Though my own red roses there may blow;
It is little I repair to the matches of the Southron folk,
Though the red roses crest the caps, I know.
For the field is full of shades as I near the shadowy coast,
And a ghostly batsman plays to the bowling of a ghost,
And I look through my tears on a soundless-clapping host
    As the run-stealers flicker to and fro,
        To and fro:—
      O my Hornby and my Barlow long ago!

Robert Blatchford
1851–1943

Robert Blatchford was a political journalist and author whose tract *Merrie England* of 1893 was a huge influence on the development of socialism in Britain. The utopian ideas from that text fed into his novel *The Sorcery Shop*, published in 1907. The book was one of many utopian fantasies of the time. The slender plot involves two MPs and businessmen, Mr Jorkle and General Storm, having a magical encounter with Mr Fry who takes them to an ideal England. Sport, play, and leisure all figure in Blatchford's utopian vision. In this extract, he contrasts the enjoyment and improvement that working people could get from their sporting lives with the 'betting and the public-house' of the real world. Blatchford also manages a dig at the animal sports that have been a key theme in this collection: they are only for the rich, he notes, with the aside 'supposing that shooting and fishing are sports'. His vision of accessible sport as being central to the culture of an ideal community has remained influential in social democratic political thinking.

"Well," said Mr. Jorkle, "but besides mending roads and digging drains, what have these people to amuse them?"

"Well, as you have seen," said Mr. Fry, "they have music and dancing."

"And, besides?"

"Well, there is art."

"But all men are not artists, nor are all men fond of music."

"True. Then we have literature and science."

"You call those amusements?"

"I do. But I will pass them by, and come to sports and pastimes. And, to begin with, there are cricket and football. These games are played all over the world. Last week England beat France, in Paris, by one wicket. This week England plays Russia in London, and Germany at Manchester. The Russians are very strong; they beat the Indians last week at Moscow, and the Indians are a very fine team."

"Good," said the General; "go on."

"Well. Besides cricket and football, there are rowing, sailing, skating, swimming, cycling, and all kinds of indoor and outdoor athletics, most of which have county championships, and international championships, attached to them. And there are baseball, lacrosse, and tennis, and golf clubs. And there are the theatres."

"All jolly good things," said the General.

"Surely," said the wizard, "and then there are all the social pleasures. Here they have picnics and festivals, for instance, with music, and games, and dancing in the open air. This week is the May Festival, and everybody goes out to enjoy the beauties and joys of the Spring."

"H'm! Sounds rather rustic; but I daresay it's all right," said the General.

"Yes," said the wizard, "these people can dance, and sing, and play, and have been taught to use their eyes. They find great delight in the skies, and fields, and flowers, and birds; and I might say they find even more delight in each other. You can understand, I am sure, General, that a young man need not feel bored by a ramble in the woods with one of the beautiful girls we saw to-night at the ball."

"Hah! By Jove!" said the General.

"Well," said the wizard, "with good health, beautiful towns and country, pleasant work, pleasant games, music, theatres, dancing, cricket, rowing, sailing, cycling, art, science, literature, and the loveliest and sweetest women ever seen surely these people need not be sad nor dull for lack of sport and occupation."

"It sounds all right," said the General.

"Oh, it *sounds* fair enough," said Mr Jorkle.

"Thank you," said the wizard. "And now, gentlemen, let us turn our attention to *our* England, and ask ourselves questions about the amusements of the people there."

"Hah! That's fair, certainly," said the General, "but what an artful customer you are, Fry. Well, you have no shootin' here, anyhow."

"And," said the wizard, "supposing that shooting and fishing are sports, how much of such sports do the people get in England now? I think you'll find that fox-hunting, and pheasant shooting, and salmon and trout fishing are sports for the well-to-do. The people never have the chance to try them."

"Hah! That's true, certainly," said the General, "but the working classes have their fun, too, I suppose."

"Well, let us see what fun they have, and how much of it," said the wizard. "First of all, you will admit—Mr. Jorkle has already admitted—that they don't get much fun out of their work. Their work is largely mechanical, a monotonous, uninteresting task, done for others, and under the orders of others, and for the advantage of others. For what art or invention is there in the work of the farm labourer, the docker, the collier, the bricksetter, the nailmaker, the factory hand, the stoker, the tailor, the seamstress, the charwoman, or the domestic servant? The great mass of the workers are merely wheels in a great machine; they are turned round and round by other wheels. Then they live in ugly and gloomy streets, and work in unhealthy and unpleasant shops or factories. And they work long hours: from eight to twelve a day. Their towns and cities are not beautiful, and they see very little of the country. Ask the men and women in our own big towns a few simple questions about trees, or birds, or flowers. There are millions of people in our England who have never seen the sea, who have hardly ever seen a wood, or a field, who have never played cricket, nor rowed a boat, nor swum fifty yards in clean water. The average British citizen does not know a titmouse from a yellow-hammer, a grayling from a chub, a beech from an elm. The average British citizen cannot sing, nor play, nor read music, nor paint, nor draw, nor carve, nor dance. The average British citizen never looks at the sky, nor at the birds nor flowers. He does not know good literature, nor art, nor drama, nor music, from bad. He could not make a picture frame, a copper tray, a silver bracelet, a kitchen poker, nor a three-legged stool. He could not cook a dinner, nor graft a slip on a tree, nor dig a straight trench, nor steer a boat, nor splice a rope, nor mend a kettle, nor break a ball from the off.

What do the masses in our towns ever see of Nature? What do the labourers in our villages ever see of art or hear of music? In our England the great bulk of the people have no artistic nor intellectual pleasures. Have you ever been to the average village concert? Have you ever been to the cheap popular music-halls and theatres? Have you ever studied the cheap popular fiction?

"With these people, in this new England, life itself is beautiful. With us life is sordid, ugly, and monotonous. For our people there are the most banal music-halls, the most fatuous plays, the most egregious novels, the cheapest music; but there are betting and the public-house.

"But the whole of this new English nation has the best literature, art, music, sport, and athletics; better than the rich with us; and besides that, these people have more culture, finer health and a greater capacity for enjoyment. Go into the crowded quarters of London, Glasgow, Manchester, and the Black Country, and see what the homes and the lives of the workers are like and how much and what manner of amusements fall to their lot; and then ask yourselves whether here, in this fair and happy England, life is dull and slow? Why, the majority of our people do not know *how* to enjoy themselves. They have only learnt to worry and to work."

"Oh, you exaggerate," said Mr. Jorkle.

"No," said the wizard, "I am speaking of things I know, and have seen. Go into the towns and see the children in the block buildings playing behind iron bars, like animals in cages. Go and watch the youth and maidens of the East End on a Bank Holiday. Go to Southend or to Blackpool, and observe a holiday crowd."

"Well, after all," said Mr. Jorkle, "life should be something more serious than a pic-nic. Work is more important than play."

The wizard laughed. "You are changing front," he said; "we were speaking about play. You had both suggested that these people here had not enough of play. But when we come to speak of work I shall try to convince you that the new England beats the old in both play and work."

"I shall be hard to convince," said Mr. Jorkle. "So far, I have seen only indications of trifling and pleasure-seeking. Music and dancing are poor equipments for the stern work of the world. I'm afraid these Utopians would fare badly in the rush and hurry of modern life."

"Ah!" said the wizard, "now you are thinking of the ruthless scuffle and fevered rush of *our* England. There is no such madness here."

E. M. FORSTER
1879–1970

Wild swimming is the name we now give to any bathing in ponds, lakes, and rivers. In E. M. Forster's classic novel *A Room with a View*, published in 1908, it was just called swimming. The novel centres on middle-class Lucy Honeychurch, and her struggles with the expectations that her family and society place on her. Sport figures in her life, with some of her courtship rituals played out on the tennis court. In this extract though, we see some of the male characters letting loose in a natural pool in the woods, with the local vicar Mr Beebe shedding his clothes and his modesty to swim, splash, and play. The unexpected arrival of some women brings Beebe and his fellow bathers back to reality, but not before they have lost the cares and inhibitions in play for its own sake. We may have rebranded natural swimming, but Forster's invocation of its charms – 'Water, sky, evergreens, a wind' – are timeless.

'Here we are!' called Freddy.

'Oh, good!' exclaimed Mr Beebe, mopping his brow.

'In there's the pond. I wish it was bigger,' he added apologetically.

They climbed down a slippery bank of pine-needles. There lay the pond, set in its little alp of green – only a pond, but large enough to contain the human body, and pure enough to reflect the sky. On account of the rains, the waters had flooded the surrounding grass, which showed like a beautiful emerald path, tempting the feet towards the central pool.

'It's distinctly successful, as ponds go,' said Mr Beebe. 'No apologies are necessary for the pond.'

George sat down where the ground was dry, and drearily unlaced his boots.

'Aren't those masses of willow-herb splendid? I love willow-herb in seed. What's the name of this aromatic plant?'

No one knew or seemed to care.

'These abrupt changes of vegetation – this little spongeous tract of water-plants, and on either side of it all the growths are tough or brittle – heather, bracken, hurts, pines. Very charming, very charming.'

'Mr Beebe, aren't you bathing?' called Freddy, as he stripped himself.

Mr Beebe thought he was not.

'Water's wonderful!' cried Freddy, prancing in.

'Water's water,' murmured George. Wetting his hair first – a sure sign of apathy – he followed Freddy into the divine, as indifferent as if he were a statue and the pond a pail of soapsuds. It was necessary to use his muscles. It was necessary to keep clean. Mr Beebe watched them, and watched the seeds of the willow-herb dance chorically above their heads.

'Apooshoo, apooshoo, apooshoo,' went Freddy, swimming for two strokes in either direction, and then becoming involved in reeds or mud.

'Is it worth it?' asked the other, Michelangelesque on the flooded margin.

The bank broke away, and he fell into the pool before he had weighed the question properly.

'Hee – poof – I've swallowed a polly-wog. Mr Beebe, water's wonderful, water's simply ripping.'

'Water's not so bad,' said George, reappearing from his plunge, and sputtering at the sun.

'Water's wonderful. Mr Beebe, do.'

'Apooshoo, kouf.'

Mr Beebe, who was hot, and who always acquiesced where possible, looked around him. He could detect no parishioners except the pine trees, rising up steeply on all sides, and gesturing to each other against the blue. How glorious it was! The world of motor-cars and Rural Deans receded illimitably. Water, sky, evergreens, a wind – these things not even the seasons can touch, and surely they lie beyond the intrusion of man?

'I may as well wash too'; and soon his garments made a third little pile on the sward, and he too asserted the wonder of the water.

It was ordinary water, nor was there very much of it, and, as Freddy said, it reminded one of swimming in a salad. The three gentlemen rotated in the pool breast high, after the fashion of the nymphs in *Götterdämmerung*. But either because the rains had given a freshness, or because the sun was shedding a most glorious heat, or because two of the gentlemen were young in years and the third young in the spirit – for some reason or other a change came over them, and they forgot Italy and Botany and Fate. They began to play. Mr Beebe and Freddy splashed each other. A little diferentially, they splashed George. He was quiet; they feared they had offended him. Then all the forces of youth burst out. He smiled, flung himself at them, splashed them, ducked them; kicked them, muddied them, and drove them out of the pool.

'Race you round it, then,' cried Freddy, and they raced in the sunshine, and George took a short cut and dirtied his shins, and had to bathe a second time. Then Mr. Beebe consented to run – a memorable sight.

They ran to get dry, they bathed to get cool, they played at being Indians in the willow-herbs and in the bracken, they bathed to get clean. And all the time three little bundles lay discreetly on the sward, proclaiming:

'No. We are what matters. Without us shall no enterprise begin. To us shall all flesh turn in the end.'

'A try! A try!' yelled Freddy, snatching up George's bundle and placing it beside an imaginary goalpost.

'Soccer rules,' George retorted, scattering Freddy's bundle with a kick.

'Goal!'

'Goal!'

'Pass!'

'Take care my watch!' cried Mr Beebe.

Clothes flew in all directions.

'Take care my hat! No, that's enough, Freddy. Dress now. No, I say!'

But the two young men were delirious. Away they twinkled into the trees, Freddy with a clerical waistcoat under his arm, George with a wide-awake hat on his dripping hair.

'That'll do!' shouted Mr Beebe, remembering that after all he was in his own parish. Then his voice changed as if every pine tree was a Rural Dean. 'Hi! Steady on! I see people coming, you fellows!'

Yells, and widening circles over the dappled earth.

'Hi! Hi! *Ladies*!'

ARNOLD BENNETT
1867–1931

Arnold Bennett is most famous for his novels of
social life in the Five Towns, based on the Potteries
region of Staffordshire. *The Card*, published in 1911,
is a classic of this genre, telling the story of local
man Denry Machin's meteoric rise from working-
class obscurity to wealth and prominence. By the
time we meet him in this extract, he has become the
Mayor of Bursley. Like all good local politicians, he
knows the importance of patronizing the local football club, and here he stages a coup to buy one of
the country's best strikers for the struggling Bursley
FC as a way of impressing the local voters. The
episode is a rejoinder to any romantic views of football at this time: in Bennett's version, local fans
don't care about 'municipal patriotism, [or] fair
play' and only want to see victories, while local wor-
thies and businessmen try to bring them those
victories through shady deals and political intrigues
in smoke-filled rooms.

from *The Card*

Not very many days afterwards the walls of Bursley called attention, by small blue and red posters (blue and red being the historic colours of the Bursley Football Club), to a public meeting, which was to be held in the Town Hall, under the presidency of the Mayor, to consider what steps could be taken to secure the future of the Bursley Football Club.

There were two 'great' football clubs in the Five Towns – Knype, one of the oldest clubs in England, and Bursley. Both were in the League, though Knype was in the first division while Bursley was only in the second. Both were, in fact, limited companies, engaged as much in the pursuit of dividends as in the practice of the one ancient and glorious sport which appeals to the reason and the heart of England. (Neither ever paid a dividend.) Both employed professionals, who, by a strange chance, were nearly all born in Scotland; and both also employed trainers who, before an important match, took the teams off to a hydropathic establishment far, far distant from any public-house. (This was called 'training'.) Now, whereas the Knype Club was struggling along fairly well, the Bursley Club had come to the end of its resources. The great football public had practically deserted it. The explanation, of course, was that Bursley had been losing too many matches. The great football public had no use for anything but victories. It would treat its players like gods – so long as they won. But when they happened to lose, the great football public simply sulked. It did not kick a man that was down; it merely ignored him, well knowing that the man could not get up without help. It cared nothing whatever for fidelity, municipal patriotism, fair play, the chances of war, or dividends on capital. If it could see victories it would pay sixpence, but it would not pay sixpence to assist at defeats.

Still, when at a special general meeting of the Bursley Football Club Limited, held at the registered office, the Coffee House, Bursley, Councillor Barlow, J.P., Chairman of the Company since the creation of the League, announced that the Directors had reluctantly come to the conclusion that they could not conscientiously embark on the dangerous risks of the approaching season, and that it was the intention of the Directors to wind up the club, in default of adequate public interest – when Bursley read this in the *Signal*, the town was certainly shocked. Was the famous club, then, to disappear for ever, and the football ground to be sold in plots, and the grand stand for firewood? The shock was so severe that the death of Alderman

Bloor (none the less a mighty figure in Bursley) had passed as a minor event.

Hence the advertisement of the meeting in the Town Hall caused joy and hope, and people said to themselves: 'Something's bound to be done; the old club can't go out like that.' And everybody grew quite sentimental. And although nothing is supposed to be capable of filling Bursley Town Hall except a political meeting and an old folk's treat, Bursley Town Hall was as near full as made no matter for the football question. Many men had cheerfully sacrificed a game of billiards and a glass of beer in order to attend it.

The Mayor, in the chair, was a mild old gentleman who knew nothing whatever about football and had probably never seen a football match; but it was essential that the meeting should have august patronage, and so the Mayor had been trapped and tamed. On the mere fact that he paid an annual subscription to the golf club, certain parties built up the legend that he was a true sportsman, with the true interests of sport in his soul.

He uttered a few phrases, such as 'the manly game', 'old associations', 'bound up with the history of England', 'splendid fellows', 'indomitable pluck', 'dogged by misfortune' (indeed, he produced quite an impression on the rude and grim audience), and then he called upon Councillor Barlow to make a statement.

Councillor Barlow, on the Mayor's right, was a different kind of man from the Mayor. He was fifty and iron-grey, with whiskers, but no moustache; short, stoutish, raspish.

He said nothing about manliness, pluck, history, or Auld Lang Syne.

He said he had given his services as Chairman to the football club for thirteen years; that he had taken up £2000 worth of shares in the Company; and that as that moment the Company's liabilities would exactly absorb its assets, his £2000 was worth exactly nothing. 'You may say,' he said, 'I've lost that £2000 in thirteen years. That is, it's the same as if I'd been steadily paying three pun' a week out of my own pocket to provide football matches that you chaps wouldn't take the trouble to go and see. That's the straight of it! What have I got for my pains? Nothing but worries and these!' (He pointed to his grey hairs.) 'And I'm not alone; there's others; and now I have to come and defend myself at a public meeting. I'm supposed not to have the best interests of football at heart. Me and my co-Directors,' he proceeded, with even a rougher raspishness, 'have warned the town again and again what would happen if the matches weren't better patronized.

And now it's happened, and now it's too late, you want to *do* something! You can't! It's too late. There's only one thing the matter with first-class football in Bursley,' he concluded, 'and it isn't the players. It's the public – it's yourselves. You're the most craven lot of tomfools that ever a big football club had to do with. When we lose a match, what do you do? Do you come and encourage us next time? No, you stop away, and leave us fifty or sixty pound out of pocket on a match, just to teach us better! Do you expect us to win every match? Why, Preston North End itself' – here he spoke solemnly, of heroes – 'Preston North End itself in its great days didn't win every match – it lost to Accrington. But did the Preston public desert it? No! *you* – You haven't got the pluck of a louse, nor the faithfulness of a cat. You've starved your football club to death, and now you call a meeting to weep and grumble. And you have the insolence to write letters to the *Signal* about bad management, forsooth! If anybody in the hall thinks he can manage this club better than me and my co-Directors have done, I may say that we hold a majority of the shares, and we'll part with the whole show to any clever person or persons who care to take it off our hands at a bargain price. That's talking.'

He sat down.

Silence fell. Even in the Five Towns a public meeting is seldom bullied as Councillor Barlow had bullied that meeting. It was aghast. Councillor Barlow had never been popular: he had merely been respected; but thenceforward he became even less popular than before.

'I'm sure we shall all find Councillor Barlow's heat quite excusable—' the Mayor diplomatically began.

'No heat at all,' the Councillor interrupted. 'Simply cold truth!'

A number of speakers followed, and nearly all of them were against the Directors. Some, with prodigious memories for every combination of players in every match that had ever been played, sought to prove by detailed instances that Councillor Barlow and his co-Directors had persistently and regularly muddled their work during thirteen industrious years. And they defended the insulted public by asserting that no public that respected itself would pay sixpence to watch the wretched football provided by Councillor Barlow. They shouted that the team wanted reconstituting, wanted new blood.

'Yes,' shouted Councillor Barlow in reply. 'And how are you going to get new blood, with transfer fees as high as they are now? You can't get even an average good player for less than £200. Where's the money to come from? Anybody want to lend a thousand or so on second debentures?'

He laughed sneeringly.

No one showed a desire to invest in second debentures of the Bursley F.C. Ltd.

Still, speakers kept harping on the necessity of new blood in the team, and then others, bolder, harped on the necessity of new blood on the board.

'Shares on sale!' cried the Councillor. 'Any buyers? Or,' he added, 'do you want something for nothing – as usual?'

At length a gentleman rose at the back of the hall.

'I don't pretend to be an expert on football,' said he, 'though I think it's a great game, but I should like to say a few words as to this question of new blood.'

The audience craned its neck.

'Will Mr Councillor Machin kindly step up to the platform?' the Mayor suggested.

And up Denry stepped.

The thought in every mind was: 'What's he going to do? What's he got up his sleeve – this time?'

'Three cheers for Machin!' people chanted gaily.

'Order!' said the Mayor.

Denry faced the audience. He was now accustomed to audiences. He said:

'If I'm not mistaken, one of the greatest modern footballers is a native of this town.'

And scores of voices yelled: 'Ay! Callear! Callear! Greatest centre forward in England!'

'Yes,' said Denry. 'Callear is the man I mean. Callear left the district, unfortunately for the district, at the age of nineteen for Liverpool. And it was not till after he left that his astounding abilities were perceived. It isn't too much to say that he made the fortune of Liverpool City. And I believe it is the fact that he scored more goals in three seasons than any other player has ever done in the League. Then, York County, which was in a tight place last year, bought him from Liverpool for a high price, and, as all the world knows, Callear had his leg broken in the first match he played for his new club. That just happened to be the ruin of the York Club, which is now quite suddenly in bankruptcy (which happily we are not), and which is disposing of its players. Gentlemen, I say that Callear ought to come back to his native town. He is fitter than ever he was, and his proper place is in his native town.'

Loud cheers.

'As captain and centre forward of the club of the Mother of the Five Towns, he would be an immense acquisition and attraction, and he would lead us to victory.'

Renewed cheers.

'And how,' demanded Councillor Barlow, jumping up angrily, 'are we to get him back to his precious native town? Councillor Machin admits that he is not an expert on football. It will probably be news to him that Aston Villa have offered £700 to York for the transfer of Callear, and Blackburn Rovers have offered £750, and they're fighting it out between 'em. Any gentleman willing to put down £800 to buy Callear for Bursley?' he sneered. 'I don't mind telling you that steam-engines and the King himself couldn't get Callear into our club.'

'Quite finished?' Denry inquired, still standing.

Laughter, overtopped by Councillor Barlow's snort as he sat down.

Denry lifted his voice.

'Mr Callear, will you be good enough to step forward and let us all have a look at you?'

The effect of these apparently simple words surpassed any effect previously obtained by the most complex flights of oratory in that hall. A young, blushing, clumsy, long-limbed, small-bodied giant stumbled along the central aisle and climbed the steps to the platform, where Denry pointed him to a seat. He was recognized by all the true votaries of the game. And everybody said to everybody: 'By Gosh! It's him, right enough. It's Callear!' And a vast astonishment and expectation of good fortune filled the hall. Applause burst forth, and though no one knew what the appearance of Callear signified, the applause continued and waxed.

'Good old Callear!' The hoarse shouts succeeded each other. 'Good old Machin!'

'Anyhow,' said Denry, when the storm was stilled, 'we've got him here, without either steam-engines or His Majesty. Will the Directors of the club accept him?'

'And what about the transfer?' Councillor Barlow demanded.

'Would you accept him and try another season if you could get him free?' Denry retorted.

Councillor Barlow always knew his mind, and was never afraid to let other people share that knowledge.

'Yes,' he said.

'Then I will see that you have the transfer free.'

'But what about York?'

'I have settled with York provisionally,' said Denry. 'That is my affair. I have returned from York today. Leave all that to me. This town has had many benefactors far more important than myself. But I shall be able to claim this originality: I'm the first to make a present of a live man to the town. Gentlemen – Mr Mayor – I venture to call for three cheers for the greatest centre forward in England, our fellow-townsman.'

The scene, as the *Signal* said, was unique.

And at the Sports Club and the other clubs afterwards, men said to each other: 'No one but him would have thought of bringing Callear over specially and showing him on the platform . . . That's cost him above twopence, that has!'

Two days later a letter appeared in the *Signal* (signed 'Fiat Justitia'), suggesting that Denry, as some reward for his public spirit, ought to be the next mayor of Bursley, in place of Alderman Bloor deceased. The letter urged that he would make an admirable mayor, the sort of mayor the old town wanted in order to wake it up. And also it pointed out that Denry would be the youngest mayor that Bursley had ever had, and probably the youngest mayor in England that year. The sentiment in the last idea appealed to the town. The town decided that it would positively *like* to have the youngest mayor it had ever had, and probably the youngest mayor in England that year. The *Signal* printed dozens of letters on the subject. When the Council met, more informally than formally, to choose a chief magistrate in place of the dead alderman, several councillors urged that what Bursley wanted was a young and *popular* mayor. And, in fine, Councillor

Barlow was shelved for a year. On the choice being published the entire town said: 'Now we *shall* have a mayoralty and don't you forget it!'

And Denry said to Nellie: 'You'll be mayoress to the youngest mayor, etc., my child. And it's cost me, including hotel and travelling expenses, eight hundred and eleven pounds six and sevenpence.'

CHARLES HAMILTON SORLEY
1895–1915

There is an awful tragedy in this poem. Charles Hamilton Sorley was only twenty years old when he was shot by a sniper in the Battle of Loos in October 1915. Published posthumously, *Marlborough and Other Poems* captured the dynamism and idealism of the schoolboy, which was quickly blunted in the grim realities of the Western Front with its 'millions of the mouthless dead'. 'The Song of the Ungirt Runners' comes from happier times, when he was a keen cross-country runner at Marlborough College in Wiltshire. The fast-moving lines speak of running for running's sake – 'we do not run for prize' – and of the transcendence that exercising carefree in nature can bring. Here, Sorley and his fellow schoolboy athletes are at one with the elements, a bitter contrast to the industrial warfare that was to kill him in his prime.

'The Song of the Ungirt Runners'

We swing ungirded hips,
And lightened are our eyes,
The rain is on our lips,
We do not run for prize.
We know not whom we trust
Nor whitherward we fare,
But we run because we must
      Through the great wide air.

The waters of the seas
Are troubled as by storm.
The tempest strips the trees
And does not leave them warm.
Does the tearing tempest pause?
Do the tree-tops ask it why?
So we run without a cause
      'Neath the big bare sky.

The rain is on our lips,
We do not run for prize.
But the storm the water whips
And the wave howls to the skies.
The winds arise and strike it
And scatter it like sand,
And we run because we like it
        Through the broad bright land.

SAKI
1870–1916

Hector Hugh Munro, who wrote under the pen name Saki, was renowned for his short stories, many of which were set in the upper-class society of his time. His sharp, satirical observations and dark humour still stand out. In this story, 'Fate', we see the lengths that Rex Dillot, one of his anti-heroes, will go to in order to protect a high stakes bet that he cannot afford to lose. Leaving aside the potentially disastrous way in which Rex saves his money, 'Fate', with its mix of billiards, bores, and braggards, is a wonderful introduction to Saki's view of the world, and to the place of casual betting amongst the leisured classes. Saki was one of the many literary talents whose life was cut short by the First World War, and 'Fate' first appeared in a posthumous collection of his stories, published three years after he was killed by a sniper on the Western Front.

'Fate'

Rex Dillot was nearly twenty-four, almost good-looking and quite penniless. His mother was supposed to make him some sort of an allowance out of what her creditors allowed her, and Rex occasionally strayed into the ranks of those who earn fitful salaries as secretaries or companions to people who are unable to cope unaided with their correspondence or their leisure. For a few months he had been assistant editor and business manager of a paper devoted to fancy mice, but the devotion had been all on one side, and the paper disappeared with a certain abruptness from club reading-rooms and other haunts where it had made a gratuitous appearance. Still, Rex lived with some air of comfort and well-being, as one can live if one is born with a genius for that sort of thing, and a kindly Providence usually arranged that his week-end invitations coincided with the dates on which his one white dinner-waistcoat was in a laundry-returned condition of dazzling cleanness. He played most games badly, and was shrewd enough to recognise the fact, but he had developed a marvellously accurate judgement in estimating the play and chances of other people, whether in a golf match, billiard handicap, or croquet tournament. By dint of parading his opinion of such and such a player's superiority with a sufficient degree of youthful assertiveness he usually succeeded in provoking a wager at liberal odds, and he looked to his week-end winnings to carry him through the financial embarrassments of his mid-week existence. The trouble was, as he confided to Clovis Sangrail, that he never had enough available or even prospective cash at his command to enable him to fix the wager at a figure really worth winning.

"Some day," he said, "I shall come across a really safe thing, a bet that simply can't go astray, and then I shall put it up for all I'm worth, or rather for a good deal more than I'm worth, or rather for a good deal more than I'm worth, if you sold me up to the last button."

"It would be awkward if it didn't happen to come off," said Clovis.

"It would be more than awkward," said Rex; "it would be a tragedy. All the same, it would be extremely amusing to bring it off. Fancy awaking in the morning with about three hundred pounds standing to one's credit. I should go and clear out my hostess's pigeon-loft before breakfast out of sheer good-temper."

"Your hostess of the moment mightn't have a pigeon-loft," said Clovis.

"I always choose hostesses that have," said Rex; "a pigeon-loft is indicative of a careless, extravagant, genial disposition, such as I like to see around me. People who strew corn broadcast for a lot of feathered inanities that just sit about cooing and giving each other the glad eye in a Louis Quatorze manner are pretty certain to do you well."

"Young Strinnit is coming down this afternoon," said Clovis reflectively; "I dare say you won't find it difficult to get him to back himself at billiards. He plays a pretty useful game, but he's not quite as good as he fancies he is."

"I know one member of the party who can walk round him," said Rex softly, an alert look coming into his eyes; "that cadaverous-looking Major who arrived last night. I've seen him play at St. Moritz. If I could get Strinnit to lay odds on himself against the Major the money would be safe in my pocket. This looks like the good thing I've been watching and praying for."

"Don't be rash," counselled Clovis, "Strinnit may play up to his self-imagined form once in a blue moon."

"I intend to be rash," said Rex quietly, and the look on his face corroborated his words.

"Are you all going to flock to the billiard-room?"

asked Teresa Thundleford, after dinner, with an air of some disapproval and a good deal of annoyance.

"I can't see what particular amusement you find in watching two men prodding little ivory balls about on a table."

"Oh, well," said her hostess, "it's a way of passing the time, you know."

"A very poor way, to my mind," said Mrs. Thundleford; "now I was going to have shown all of you the photographs I took in Venice last summer."

"You showed them to us last night," said Mrs. Cuvering hastily.

"Those were the ones I took in Florence. These are quite a different lot."

"Oh, well, some time to-morrow we can look at them. You can leave them down in the drawing-room, and then every one can have a look."

"I should prefer to show them when you are all gathered together, as I have quite a lot of explanatory remarks to make, about Venetian art and architecture, on the same lines as my remarks last night on the Florentine galleries. Also, there are some verses of mine that I should like to read you, on the rebuilding of the Campanile. But, of course, if you all prefer to watch Major Latton and Mr. Strinnit knocking balls about on a table——"

"They are both supposed to be first-rate players," said the hostess.

"I have yet to learn that my verses and my art *causerie* are of second-rate quality," said Mrs. Thundleford with acerbity. "However, as you all seem bent on watching a silly game, there's no more to be said. I shall go upstairs and finish some writing. Later on, perhaps, I will come down and join you."

To one, at least, of the onlookers the game was anything but silly. It was absorbing, exciting, exasperating, nerve-stretching, and finally it grew to be tragic. The Major with the St. Moritz reputation was playing a long way below his form, young Strinnit was playing slightly above his, and had all the luck of the game as well. From the very start the balls seemed possessed by a demon of contrariness; they trundled about complacently for one player, they would go nowhere for the other.

"A hundred and seventy, seventy-four," sang out the youth who was marking. In a game of two hundred and fifty up it was an enormous lead to hold. Clovis watched the flush of excitement die away from Dillot's face, and a hard white look take its place.

"How much have you got on?" whispered Clovis. The other whispered the sum through dry, shaking lips. It was more than he or any one connected with him could pay; he had done what he had said he would do. He had been rash.

"Two hundred and six, ninety-eight."

Rex heard a clock strike ten somewhere in the hall, then another somewhere else, and another, and another; the house seemed full of striking clocks. Then in the distance the stable clock chimed in. In another hour they would all be striking eleven, and he would be listening to them as a disgraced outcast, unable to pay, even in part, the wager he had challenged.

"Two hundred and eighteen, a hundred and three." The game was as good as over. Rex was as good as done for. He longed desperately for the ceiling to fall in, for the house to catch fire, for anything to happen that would put an end to that horrible rolling to and fro of red and white ivory that was jostling him nearer and nearer to his doom.

"Two hundred and twenty-eight, a hundred and seven."

Rex opened his cigarette-case; it was empty. That at least gave him a pretext to slip away from the room for the purpose of refilling it; he would spare himself the drawn-out torture of watching that hopeless game played out to the bitter end. He backed away from the circle of absorbed watchers and made his way up a short stairway to a long, silent corridor of bedrooms, each with a guest's name written in a little square on the door. In the hush that reigned in this part of the house he could still hear the hateful click-click of the balls; if he waited for a few minutes longer he would hear the little outbreak of clapping and buzz of congratulation that would hail Strinnit's victory. On the alert tension of his nerves there broke another sound, the aggressive, wrath-inducing breathing of one who sleeps in heavy after-dinner slumber. The sound came from a room just at his elbow; the card on the door bore the announcement "Mrs. Thundleford." The door was just slightly ajar; Rex pushed it open an inch or two more and looked in. The august Teresa had fallen asleep over an illustrated guide to Florentine art-galleries; at her side, somewhat dangerously near the edge of the table, was a reading-lamp. If Fate had been decently kind to him, thought Rex, bitterly, that lamp would have been knocked over by the sleeper and would have given them something to think of besides billiard matches.

There are occasions when one must take one's Fate in one's hands. Rex took the lamp in his.

"Two hundred and thirty-seven, one hundred and fifteen." Strinnit was at the table, and the balls lay in good position for him; he had a choice of two fairly easy shots, a choice which he was never to decide. A sudden hurricane of shrieks and a rush of stumbling feet sent every one flocking to the door. The Dillot boy crashed into the room, carrying in his arms the vociferous and somewhat dishevelled Teresa Thundleford; her clothing was certainly not a mass of flames, as the more excitable members of the party afterwards declared, but the edge of her skirt and part of the table-cover in which she had been hastily wrapped were alight in a flickering, half-hearted manner. Rex flung his struggling burden on to the billiard table, and for one breathless minute the work of beating out the sparks with rugs and cushions and playing on them with soda-water syphons engrossed the energies of the entire company.

"It was lucky I was passing when it happened," panted Rex; "some one had better see to the room, I think the carpet is alight."

As a matter of fact the promptitude and energy of the rescuer had prevented any great damage being done, either to the victim or her surroundings. The billiard table had suffered most, and had to be laid up for repairs; perhaps it was not the best place to have chosen for the scene of salvage operations; but then, as Clovis remarked, when one is rushing about with a blazing woman in one's arms one can't stop to think out exactly where one is going to put her.

J. B. PRIESTLEY
1894–1984

Yorkshire-born novelist, playwright, and broadcaster
J. B. Priestley excelled in exploring the cultures of
people and places, and it is no surprise that one of
the most famous passages on football in English
literature came from his pen. *The Good Companions*
of 1929 follows Jess Oakroyd as he leaves the
depressed mill town of Bruddersford (based on
Priestley's home town of Bradford) to find a new
life. In the opening section, Priestley used a football
match to set the scene of the working town that
Oakroyd leaves behind. Everything about this
extract resonates for anyone who has ever felt a
sense of belonging in a sports crowd, 'a new community . . . cheering together, thumping one another
in the shoulders.' His argument that football offers
the spectator 'Conflict and Art' for the price of a
shilling shows his innate appreciation of how sport
fitted into industrial towns and their culture.

from *The Good Companions*

Yes, it is Bruddersford. Over there is the enormous factory of Messrs Holdsworth and Co. Ltd, which has never been called a noble building in any style but nevertheless looks as if it had a perfect right to be there. The roof of the Midland Railway Station glitters in the sun, and not very far away is another glitter from the glass roof of the Bruddersford Market Hall, where, securely under cover, you may have a ham tea or buy boots and pans and mint humbugs and dress lengths and comic songs. That squat bulk to the left of the Town Hall is the Lane End Congregational Chapel, a monster that can swallow any two thousand people who happen to be in search of 'hearty singing and a bright service.' That streak of slime must be the Leeds and Liverpool Canal or the Aire and Calder Canal, one of the two. There is a little forest of mill chimneys. Most of them are only puffing meditatively, for it is Saturday afternoon and nearly four hours since the workpeople swarmed out through the big gates. Some of the chimneys show no signs of smoke; they have been quiet for a long time, have stayed there like monuments of an age that has vanished, and all because trade is still bad. Perhaps some of these chimneys have stopped smoking because fashionable women in Paris and London and New York have cried to one another, 'My dear, you can't possibly wear that!' and less fashionable women have repeated it after them, and quite unfashionable women have finally followed their example, and it has all ended in machines lying idle in Bruddersford. Certainly, trade is still very bad. But as you look down on Bruddersford, you feel that it will do something about it, that it is only biding its time, that it will hump its way through somehow: the place wears a grim and resolute look. Yet this afternoon it is not thinking about the wool trade.

Something very queer is happening in that narrow thoroughfare to the west of the town. It is called Manchester Road because it actually leads you to that city, though in order to get there you will have to climb to the windy roof of England and spend an hour or two with the curlews. What is so queer about it now is that the road itself cannot be seen at all. A grey-green tide flows sluggishly down its length. It is a tide of cloth caps.

These caps have just left the ground of the Bruddersford United Association Football Club. Thirty-five thousand men and boys have just seen what most of them call 't'United' play Bolton Wanderers. Many of them should never have been there at all. It would not be difficult to prove by statistics and those mournful little budgets (How a Man May Live – or rather, avoid death – on Thirty-five Shillings a Week) that seem to attract some minds, that these fellows could not afford the entrance fee. When some mills are only working half the week and others not at all, a shilling is a respectable sum of money. It would puzzle an economist to discover where all these shillings came from. But if he lived in Bruddersford, though he might still wonder where they came from, he would certainly understand why they were produced. To say that these men paid their shillings to watch twenty-two hirelings kick a ball is merely to say that a violin is wood and catgut, that *Hamlet* is so much paper and ink. For a shilling the Bruddersford United A.F.C. offered you Conflict and Art; it turned you into a critic, happy in your judgement of fine points, ready in a second to estimate the worth of a well-judged pass, a run down the touch line, a lightning shot, a clearance kick by back or goalkeeper; it turned you into a partisan, holding your breath when the ball came sailing into your own goalmouth, ecstatic when your forwards raced away towards the opposite goal, elated, downcast, bitter, triumphant by turns at the fortunes of your side, watching a ball shape Iliads and Odysseys for you; and, what is more, it turned you into a member of a new community, all brothers together for an hour and a half, for not only had you escaped from the clanking machinery of this lesser life, from work, wages, rent, doles, sick pay, insurance cards, nagging wives, ailing children, bad bosses, idle workmen, but you had escaped with most of your mates and your neighbours, with half the town, and there you were, cheering together, thumping one another on the shoulders, swopping judgements like lords of the earth, having pushed your way through a turn-stile into another and altogether more splendid kind of life, hurtling with Conflict and yet passionate and beautiful in its Art. Moreover, it offered you more than a shilling's worth of material for talk during the rest of the week. A man who had missed the last home match of 't'United' had to enter social life on tiptoe in Bruddersford.

A. G. MACDONELL
1895–1941

England, Their England, published in 1933, is Scottish
novelist A. G. Macdonell's satire on English society
as seen by an outsider. The protagonist, Donald
Cameron, is a Scot, like his creator. He lives in England for a year, and reports on his varied encounters
with the English at work, in politics, and, of course,
at play. The village cricket match that he finds himself playing is perhaps the novel's most famous
sporting episode, but this extract, based at Cedar
Park golf club, offers comedy value and keen observations on the pretensions and habits of the English
business class. Macdonell contrasts Cameron's natural golfing ability with the over-complicated play of
the English, who are more interested in showing
off their wealth and their equipment than in mastering the game. Back in the clubhouse, it is clear to
Cameron that betting, eating, drinking, and dressing
to impress are all far more important in this country
club atmosphere than the simple pleasures of playing a round.

from *England, Their England*

Cedar Park is one of the newest of the great golf clubs which are ringed round the north, west, and south of London in such profusion, and what is now the club-house had been in earlier centuries the mansion of a venerable line of marquesses. High taxation had completed the havoc in the venerable finances which had been begun in the Georgian and Victorian generations by high gambling, and the entire estate was sold shortly after the War by the eleventh marquess to a man who had, during it, made an enormous fortune by a most ingenious dodge. For, alone with the late Lord Kitchener, he had realized in August and September of 1914 that the War was going to be a very long business, thus providing ample opportunities for very big business, and that before it was over it would require a British Army of millions and millions of soldiers. Having first of all taken the precaution of getting himself registered as a man who was indispensable to the civil life of the nation during the great Armageddon, for at the outbreak of hostilities he was only thirty-one years of age, and, in order to be on the safe side, having had himself certified by a medical man as suffering from short sight, varicose veins, a weak heart, and incipient lung trouble, he set himself upon his great task of cornering the world's supply of rum. By the middle of 1917 he had succeeded, and in 1920 he paid ninety-three thousand pounds for Cedar Park, and purchased in addition a house in Upper Brook Street, a hunting-box near Melton, a two-thousand-ton motor-yacht, Lochtarig Castle, Inverness-shire, and the long leases of three luxurious flats in Mayfair in which to entertain, without his wife knowing, by day or night, his numerous lady friends. He was, of course, knighted for his public services during the War. It was not until 1925 that the rum-knight shot himself to avoid an absolutely certain fourteen years for fraudulent conversion, and Cedar Park was acquired by a syndicate of Armenian sportsmen for the purpose of converting it into a country club.

An enormous man in a pale-blue uniform tricked out with thick silver cords and studded with cart-wheel silver buttons, opened the door of the car and bowed Sir Ludovic, and a little less impressively, Donald Cameron into the club-house. Donald was painfully conscious that his grey flannel trousers bagged at the knee and that his old blue 1914 golfing-coat had a shine at one elbow and a hole at the other.

The moment he entered the club-house a superb spectacle met his dazzled gaze. It was not the parquet floor, on which his nail-studded shoes squeaked loudly, or the marble columns, or the voluptuous paintings on the ceiling, or the gilt-framed mirrors on the walls, or the chandeliers of a thousand crystals, or even the palms in their gilt pots and synthetic earth, that knocked him all of a heap. It was the group of golfers that was standing in front of the huge fire-place. There were purple jumpers and green jumpers and yellow jumpers and tartan jumpers; there were the biggest, the baggiest, the brightest plus-fours that ever dulled the lustre of a peacock's tail; there were the rosiest of lips, the gayest of cheeks, the flimsiest of silk stockings, and the orangest of finger-nails and probably, if the truth were known, of toe-nails too; there were waves of an unbelievable permanence and lustre; there were jewels, on the men as well as on the women, and foot-long jade and amber cigarette-holders and foot-long cigars with glistening cummerbunds; and there was laughter and gaiety and much bending, courtier-like, from the waist, and much raising of girlish, kohl-fringed eyes, and a great chattering. Donald felt like a navvy, and when, in his agitation, he dropped his clubs with a resounding clash upon the floor and everyone stopped talking and looked at him, he wished he was dead. Another pale-blue-and-silver giant picked up the clubs, held them out at arm's length and examined them in disdainful astonishment – for after years of disuse they were very rusty – and said coldly, 'Clubs go into the locker-room, sir,' and Donald squeaked his way across the parquet after him amid a profound silence.

The locker-room was full of young gentlemen who were discarding their jumpers – which certainly competed with Mr Shelley's idea of Life Staining the White Radiance of Eternity – in favour of brown leather jerkins fastened up the front with that singular arrangement which is called a zipper. Donald edged in furtively, hazily watched the flunkey lay the clubs down upon a bench, and then fled in panic through the nearest open door and found himself suddenly in a wire-netted enclosure which was packed with a dense throng of caddies. The caddies were just as surprised by his appearance in their midst as the elegant ladies and gentlemen in the lounge had been by the fall of the clubs, and a deathly stillness once again paralysed Donald.

He backed awkwardly out of the enclosure, bouncing off caddy after caddy like a cork coming over a rock-studded sluice, and was brought up short at last by what seemed to be a caddy rooted immovably in the ground. Two desperate backward lunges failed to dislodge the obstacle and Donald turned and found it was the wall of the professional's shop. The caddies, and worse still, an exquisitely beautiful young lady with a cupid's-bow mouth and practically no skirt on at all, who had just emerged from the shop, watched him with profound interest. Scarlet in the face, he rushed past the radiant beauty, and hid himself in the darkest corner of the shop and pretended to be utterly absorbed in a driver which he picked out at random from the rack. Rather to his surprise, and greatly to his relief, no one molested him with up-to-date, go-getting salesmanship, and in a few minutes he had pulled himself together and was able to look round and face the world.

Suddenly he gave a start. Something queer was going on inside him. He sniffed the air once, and then again, and then the half-forgotten past came rushing to him across the wasted years. The shining rows of clubs, the boxes of balls, the scent of leather and rubber and gripwax and pitch, the club-makers filing away over the vices and polishing and varnishing and splicing and binding, the casual members waggling a club here and there, the professional listening courteously to tales of apocryphal feats, all the old familiar scenes of his youth came back to him. It was eleven years since he had played a game of golf, thirteen years since he had bought a club.

Thirteen wasted years. Dash it, thought Donald, damn it, blast it, I can't afford a new club – I don't want a new club, but I'm going to buy a new club. He spoke diffidently to one of the assistants who was passing behind him, and inquired the price of the drivers.

'It's a new lot just finished, sir,' said the assistant, 'and I'm not sure of the price. I'll ask Mr Glennie.'

Mr Glennie was the professional himself. The great man, who was talking to a member, or rather was listening to a member's grievances against his luck, a ritual which occupied a large part of a professional's working day, happened to overhear the assistant, and he said over his shoulder in the broadest of broad Scottish accents, 'They're fufty-twa shullin' and cheap at that.'

Donald started back. Two pounds twelve for a driver! Things had changed indeed since the days when the great Archie Simpson had sold him a brassy, brand-new, bright yellow, refulgent, with a lovely whippy shaft, for five shillings and ninepence.

His movement of Aberdonian horror brought him out of the dark corner into the sunlight which was streaming through the window, and it was the professional's turn to jump.

'It's Master Donald!' he exclaimed. 'Ye mind me, Master Donald – Jim Glennie, assistant that was at

Glenavie to Tommy Anderson that went to the States?'

'Glennie!' cried Donald, a subtle warm feeling suddenly invading his body, and he grasped the professional's huge red hand.

'Man!' cried the latter, 'but I'm glad to see ye. How lang is't sin' we used to ding awa at each other roon' Glenavie? Man, it must be years and years. And fit's aye deein' wi' yer game? Are ye plus sax or seeven?'

'Glennie,' said Donald sadly, 'I haven't touched a club since those old days. This is the first time I've set foot in a professional's shop since you took me that time to see Alex Marling at Balgownie the day before the War broke out.'

'Eh, man, but you're a champion lost,' and the professional shook his head mournfully.

'But, Glennie,' went on Donald, 'where did you learn that fine Buchan accent? You never used to talk like that. Is it since you came south that you've picked it up?'

The big professional looked a little shamefaced and drew Donald back into the dark corner.

'It's good for trade,' he whispered in the pure English of Inverness. 'They like a Scot to be real Scottish. They think it makes a man what they call "a character". God knows why, but there it is. So I just humour them by talking like a Guild Street carter who's having a bit of back-chat with an Aberdeen fish-wife. It makes the profits something extraordinary.'

'Hi! Glennie, you old swindler,' shouted a stoutish red-faced man who was smoking a big cigar and wearing a spectroscopic suit of tweeds. 'How much do you want to sting me for this putter?'

'Thirty-twa shullin' and saxpence, Sir Walter,' replied Glennie over his shoulder, 'but ye'll be wastin' yer siller, for neither that club nor any ither wull bring ye doon below eighteen.'

A delighted laugh from a group of men behind Sir Walter greeted this sally.

'You see,' whispered Glennie, 'he'll buy it and he'll tell his friends that I tried to dissuade him, and they'll agree that I'm a rare old character, and they'll all come and buy too.'

'But fifty-two shillings for a driver!' said Donald. 'Do you mean to say they'll pay that?'

'Yes, of course they will. They'll pay anything so long as it's more than any other professional at any other club charges them. That's the whole secret. Those drivers there aren't a new set at all. They're the same set as I was asking forty-eight shillings for last weekend, but I heard during the week from a friend who keeps an eye open for me, that young

Jock Robbie over at Addingdale Manor had put his drivers and brassies up from forty-six shillings to fifty, the dirty young dog. Not that I blame him. It's a new form of commercial competition, Master Donald, a sort of inverted price-cutting. Na, na, Muster Hennessey,' he broke into his trade voice again, 'ye dinna want ony new clubs. Ye're playin' brawly with yer auld yins. Still, if ye want to try yon spoon, tak it oot and play a couple of roons wi' it, and if ye dinna like it put it back.'

He turned to Donald again.

'That's a sure card down here. They always fall for it. They take the club and tell their friends that I've given it to them on trial because I'm not absolutely certain that it will suit their game, and they never bring it back. Not once. Did you say you wanted a driver, Master Donald?'

'Not at fifty-two shillings,' said Donald with a smile.

Glennie indignantly waved away the suggestion.

'You shall have your pick of the shop at cost price,' he said, and then, looking furtively round and lowering his voice until it was almost inaudible, he breathed in Donald's ear, 'Fifteen and six.'

Donald chose a beautiful driver, treading on air all the while and feeling eighteen years of age, and then Sir Ludovic Phibbs came into the shop.

'Ah! There you are, Cameron,' he said genially; 'there are only two couples in front of us now. Are you ready? Good morning, Glennie, you old shark. There's no use trying to swing the lead over Mr Cameron. He's an Aberdonian himself.'

As Donald went out, Glennie thrust a box of balls under his arm and whispered, 'For old times' sake!'

On the first tee Sir Ludovic introduced him to the other two players who were going to make up the match. One was a Mr Wollaston, a clean-shaven, intelligent, large, prosperous-looking man of about forty, and the other was a Mr Gyles, a very dark man, with a toothbrush moustache and a most impressive silence. Both were stockbrokers.

'Now,' said Sir Ludovic heartily, 'I suggest that we play a fourball foursome, Wollaston and I against you two, on handicap, taking our strokes from the course, five bob corners, half a crown for each birdie, a dollar an eagle, a bob best ball and a bob aggregate and a bob a putt. What about that?'

'Good!' said Mr Wollaston. Mr Gyles nodded, while Donald, who had not understood a single word except the phrase 'four-ball foursome' – and that was incorrect – mumbled a feeble affirmative. The stakes sounded enormous, and the reference to birds of the air sounded mysterious, but he obviously could not raise any objections.

When it was his turn to drive at the first tee, he selected a spot for his tee and tapped it with the toe of his driver. Nothing happened. He looked at his elderly caddy and tapped the ground again. Again nothing happened.

'Want a peg, Cameron?' called out Sir Ludovic.

'Oh no, it's much too early,' protested Donald, under the impression that he was being offered a drink. Everyone laughed ecstatically at this typically Scottish flash of wit, and the elderly caddy lurched forward with a loathsome little contrivance of blue and white celluloid which he offered to his employer. Donald shuddered. They'd be giving him a rubber tee with a tassel in a minute, or lending him a golf-bag with tripod legs. He teed his ball on a pinch of sand with a dexterous twist of his fingers and thumb amid an incredulous silence.

Donald played the round in a sort of daze. After a few holes of uncertainty, much of his old skill came back, and he reeled off fairly good figures. He had a little difficulty with his elderly caddy at the beginning of the round, for, on asking that functionary to hand him 'the iron', he received the reply, 'Which number, sir?' and the following dialogue ensued:

'Which number what?' faltered Donald.

'Which number iron?'

'Er – just the iron.'

'But it must have a number, sir.'

'Why must it?'

'All irons have numbers.'

'But I've only one.'

'Only a number one?'

'No. Only one.'

'Only one what, sir?'

'One iron!' exclaimed Donald, feeling that this music-hall turn might go on for a long time and must be already holding up the entire course.

The elderly caddy at last appreciated the deplorable state of affairs. He looked grievously shocked and said in a reverent tone:

'Mr Fumbledon has eleven.'

'Eleven what?' inquired the startled Donald.

'Eleven irons.'

After this revelation of Mr Fumbledon's greatness, Donald took 'the iron' and topped the ball hard along the ground. The caddy sighed deeply.

Throughout the game Donald never knew what the state of the match was, for the other three, who kept complicated tables upon the backs of envelopes, reckoned solely in cash. Thus, when Donald once timidly asked his partner how they stood, the taciturn Mr Gyles consulted his envelope and replied shortly, after a brief calculation, 'You're up three dollars and a tanner.'

Donald did not venture to ask again, and he knew nothing more about the match until they were ranged in front of the bar in the club-room, when Sir Ludovic and Mr Wollaston put down the empty glasses which had, a moment ago, contained double pink gins, ordered a refill of the four glasses, and then handed over to the bewildered Donald the sum of one pound sixteen and six.

Lunch was an impressive affair. It was served in a large room, panelled in white and gold with a good deal of artificial marble scattered about the walls, by a staff of bewitching young ladies in black frocks, white aprons and caps, and black silk stockings. Bland wine-stewards drifted hither and thither, answering to Christian names and accepting orders and passing them on to subordinates. Corks popped, the scent of the famous club fish-pie mingled itself with all the perfumes of Arabia and Mr Coty, smoke arose from rose-tipped cigarettes, and the rattle of knives and forks played an orchestral accompaniment to the sound of many voices, mostly silvery, like April rain, and full of girlish gaiety.

Sir Ludovic insisted on being host, and ordered Donald's half-pint of beer and double whiskies for himself and Mr Gyles. Mr Wollaston, pleading a diet and the strict orders of Carlsbad medicos, produced a bottle of Berncastler out of a small brown hand-bag, and polished it off in capital style.

The meal itself consisted of soup, the famous fish-pie, a fricassee of chicken, saddle of mutton or sirloin of roast beef, sweet, savoury, and cheese, topped off with four of the biggest glasses of hunting port that Donald had ever seen. Conversation at lunch was almost entirely about the dole. The party then went back to the main club-room where Mr Wollaston firmly but humorously pushed Sir Ludovic into a very deep chair, and insisted upon taking up the running with four coffees and four double kümmels. Then after a couple of rubbers of bridge, at which Donald managed to win a few shillings, they sallied out to play a second round. The golf was only indifferent in the afternoon. Sir Ludovic complained that, owing to the recrudes-cence of what he mysteriously called 'the old trouble', he was finding it very difficult to focus the ball clearly, and Mr Wollaston kept on over-swinging so violently that he fell over once and only just saved himself on several other occasions, and Mr Gyles developed a fit of socketing that soon became a menace to the course, causing, as it did, acute nerv-ous shocks to a retired major-general whose sunlit nose only escaped by a miracle, and a bevy of beauty that was admiring, for some reason, the play of a well-known actor-manager.

So after eight holes the afternoon round was abandoned by common consent, and they walked back to the club-house for more bridge and much-needed refreshment. Donald was handed seventeen shillings as his inexplicable winnings over the eight holes. Later on, Sir Ludovic drove, or rather Sir Ludovic's chauffeur drove, Donald back to the corner of King's Road and Royal Avenue. On the way back, Sir Ludovic talked mainly about the dole. Seated in front of the empty grate in his bed-sitting-room, Donald counted his winnings and reflected that golf had changed a great deal since he had last played it.

WINIFRED HOLTBY
1898–1935

In her classic novel *South Riding*, published posthumously in 1936, feminist and pacifist author Winifred Holtby dealt with many key social issues of the inter-war period, including education, poverty, and women's roles in public life. The First World War casts a shadow over the characters, concentrated in the Cold Harbour Colony of ex-servicemen's allotments. One of these men, Bill Heyer, lost his arm at the Battle of Passchendaele. In this extract, Heyer and his friends visit the music hall, and the weight-lifting exploits of Sacho the Strong remind Heyer of his loss. He recalls all the sports he played in the army, and the camaraderie of the football pitch and the boxing ring, a culture lost to him with his arm. Sport has long been a location for male bonding. The poignancy of Holtby's visceral prose here reminds us of how fragile those bonds could be once injury and disability break them. This piece is a bitter twist on the idealistic and naive runners of Sorley's pre-war poem.

from *South Riding*

The Jewish comedienne and her ponies pranced away. A strong man replaced them, who bent bars of iron and lifted pianos, and hung upside down from a trapeze with a rod suspended from his mouth on to which more and yet more weights were slung.

A strong man, not only strong but agile, his muscles flexible as elastic and tough as steel. Heyer, whose shoulder had been aching all day since he stood on the damp football ground, thought of his own maimed body. As Hicks was bereaved of Carne, of horses, of the old values and loyalties which composed his world, Heyer was bereaved of more than his physical capacity. He too had lost a way of life, a set of values.

He knew that war was evil. With the British Legion he had passed resolutions about profiting from death and all the rest of it. But as he watched Sacho the Strong flex his huge muscles, and shouted applause at his spectacular feats, his mind was back in the worst experience of the war, the mud of Passchendaele. His feet again groped for the duck-boards through the foetid water. He was carrying rations up to the front-line trenches; the pack ground into his shoulder, the foul ooze seeped through puttees and boots. The fear of falling into that filth tormented him. Yet as he sat in his plush tip-up seat, leaning over the parapet into the boiling cauldron of the Kingsport Empire, he envied that younger self. He suffered from a sick nostalgia for the young Bob Heyer who had been Scotty's friend, who had two good arms, who could himself play football instead of watching it, who could box, swim, dig, and was one of the best all-round athletes in the company. It was Scotty who had gone down into the mud, and for whose body they had groped in the stench and ordure of a flooded crater. Nothing in all his life had been so horrible as that ... yet until he got his blighty he had known good times again. Boxing at the base; the ring in the tent at Amiens. The acid sweaty smell of men crowded together in woollen uniforms, the arc lights, the referee. The sing songs in that estaminet near Abbeville. The relief from responsibility, the good fellowship, the pride of manhood and living that grew up there in France under the menace of death. He hungered for it. He knew that all other years must be lifeless and dull compared with those. He would continue to farm. He had his friends, Tom and Geordie. He would spend his evenings when he could in the Nag's Head. But something more than his arm had been left behind in France. He would walk now maimed and bereaved till death.

JOHN BETJEMAN
1906–1984

John Betjeman was something of a national treasure, a status assured when he served as Poet Laureate from 1972 until his death. His prolific output over four decades dealt with class, character, place, Christianity, and architecture. Sport occurs in many of his poems, sometimes as the main subject, and sometimes a lens through which to study his characters. 'A Subaltern's Love-song', published in 1941, is a classic of this strand. In it, we witness a budding romance develop between the titular army officer and 'Miss Joan Hunter Dunn', a courtship played out in the tennis and golf clubs of Hampshire and Surrey. There is a restrained eroticism to the narrator's description of Joan's style of play, and the 'strenuous singles' of the tennis court are euphemistic, to say the least. Tennis matches, the golf club dance, colonial prints on the wall, gin and lime: Betjeman's eye for the detail of the culture in which this love affair develops is perfect.

'A Subaltern's Love-song'

Miss J. Hunter Dunn, Miss J. Hunter Dunn,
Furnish'd and burnish'd by Aldershot sun,
What strenuous singles we played after tea,
We in the tournament—you against me!

Love-thirty, love-forty, oh! weakness of joy,
The speed of a swallow, the grace of a boy,
With carefullest carelessness, gaily you won,
I am weak from your loveliness, Joan Hunter Dunn.

Miss Joan Hunter Dunn, Miss Joan Hunter Dunn,
How mad I am, sad I am, glad that you won.
The warm-handled racket is back in its press,
But my shock-headed victor, she loves me no less.

Her father's euonymus shines as we walk,
And swing past the summer-house, buried in talk,
And cool the verandah that welcomes us in
To the six-o'clock news and a lime-juice and gin.

The scent of the conifers, sound of the bath,
The view from my bedroom of moss-dappled path,
As I struggle with double-end evening tie,
For we dance at the Golf Club, my victor and I.

On the floor of her bedroom lie blazer and shorts
And the cream-coloured walls are be-trophied with sports,
And westering, questioning settles the sun
On your low-leaded window, Miss Joan Hunter Dunn.

The Hillman is waiting, the light's in the hall,
The pictures of Egypt are bright on the wall,
My sweet, I am standing beside the oak stair
And there on the landing's the light on your hair.

By roads "not adopted", by woodlanded ways,
She drove to the club in the late summer haze,
Into nine-o'clock Camberley, heavy with bells
And mushroomy, pine-woody, evergreen smells.

Miss Joan Hunter Dunn, Miss Joan Hunter Dunn,
I can hear from the car-park the dance has begun.
Oh! full Surrey twilight! importunate band!
Oh! strongly adorable tennis-girl's hand!

Around us are Rovers and Austins afar,
Above us, the intimate roof of the car,
And here on my right is the girl of my choice,
With the tilt of her nose and the chime of her voice,

And the scent of her wrap, and the words never said,
And the ominous, ominous dancing ahead.
We sat in the car park till twenty to one
And now I'm engaged to Miss Joan Hunter Dunn.

GEORGE ORWELL
1903–1950

George Orwell, novelist and essayist, was one of the most significant political writers and broadcasters of the twentieth century. His novels *Animal Farm* and *Nineteen Eighty-Four* remain classic explorations of totalitarianism, while his journalism touched on all aspects of politics and culture. It is fitting to end this collection with his critique of international sport, 'The Sporting Spirit', published in *Tribune* in 1945. His musings on the damage that overly nationalist sport could cause were prompted by Moscow Dynamo's goodwill tour of Britain just after the war. He uses this to reflect on sport's historical development, and on the differences between the friendly rivalry of the village green and the 'war minus the shooting' of international sport. Orwell was prescient here: the role that the Olympic Games took on as a proxy battlefield during the Cold War fits perfectly with his analysis. 'The Sporting Spirit' sums up the changes that sport has gone through since Shakespeare's wrestling match, while also reminding us that sport has always been about rivalry, identity, and excitement.

'The Sporting Spirit'

Now that the brief visit of the Dynamo football team has come to an end, it is possible to say publicly what many thinking people were saying privately before the Dynamos ever arrived. That is, that sport is an unfailing cause of ill-will, and that if such a visit as this had any effect at all on Anglo-Soviet relations, it could only be to make them slightly worse than before.

Even the newspapers have been unable to conceal the fact that at least two of the four matches played led to much bad feeling. At the Arsenal match, I am told by someone who was there, a British and a Russian player came to blows and the crowd booed the referee. The Glasgow match, someone else informs me, was simply a free-for-all from the start. And then there was the controversy, typical of our nationalistic age, about the composition of the Arsenal team. Was it really an all-England team, as claimed by the Russians, or merely a league team, as claimed by the British? And did the Dynamos end their tour abruptly in order to avoid playing an all-England team? As usual, everyone answers these questions according to his political predilections. Not quite everyone, however. I noted with interest, as an instance of the vicious passions that football provokes, that the sporting correspondent of the russophile *News Chronicle* took the anti-Russian line and maintained that Arsenal was *not* an all-England team. No doubt the controversy will continue to echo for years in the footnotes of history books. Meanwhile the result of the Dynamos' tour, in so far as it has had any result, will have been to create fresh animosity on both sides.

And how could it be otherwise? I am always amazed when I hear people saying that sport creates goodwill between the nations, and that if only the common peoples of the world could meet one another at football or cricket, they would have no inclination to meet on the battlefield. Even if one didn't know from concrete examples (the 1936 Olympic Games, for instance) that international sporting contests lead to orgies of hatred, one could deduce it from general principles.

Nearly all the sports practised nowadays are competitive. You play to win, and the game has little meaning unless you do your utmost to win. On the village green, where you pick up sides and no feeling of local patriotism is involved, it is possible to play simply for the fun and exercise: but as soon as the question of prestige arises, as soon as you feel that you and some larger unit will be disgraced if you lose, the most savage combative instincts are aroused. Anyone who has played even in a school football match knows this. At the international level sport is frankly mimic warfare. But the significant thing is not the behaviour of the players but the attitude of the spectators: and, behind the spectators, of the nations who work themselves into furies over these absurd contests, and seriously believe – at any rate for short periods – that running, jumping and kicking a ball are tests of national virtue.

Even a leisurely game like cricket, demanding grace rather than strength, can cause much ill-will, as we saw in the controversy over body-line bowling and over the rough tactics of the Australian team that visited England in 1921. Football, a game in which everyone gets hurt and every nation has its own style of play which seems unfair to foreigners, is far worse. Worst of all is boxing. One of the most horrible sights in the world is a fight between white and coloured boxers before a mixed audience. But a boxing audience is always disgusting, and the behaviour of the women, in particular, is such that the army, I believe, does not allow them to attend its contests. At any rate, two or three years ago, when Home Guards and regular troops were holding a boxing tournament, I was placed on guard at the door of the hall, with orders to keep the women out.

In England, the obsession with sport is bad enough, but even fiercer passions are aroused in young countries where games playing and nationalism are both recent developments. In countries like India or Burma, it is necessary at football matches to have strong cordons of police to keep the crowd from invading the field. In Burma, I have seen the supporters of one side break through the police and disable the goalkeeper of the opposing side at a critical moment. The first big football match that was played in Spain about fifteen years ago led to an uncontrollable riot. As soon as strong feelings of rivalry are aroused, the notion of playing the game according to the rules always vanishes. People want to see one side on top and the other side humiliated, and they forget that victory gained through cheating or through the intervention of the crowd is meaningless. Even when the spectators don't intervene physically they try to influence the game by cheering their own side and 'rattling' opposing players with boos and insults. Serious sport has nothing to do with fair play. It is bound up with hatred, jealousy, boastfulness, disregard of all rules and sadistic pleasure in witnessing violence: in other words it is war minus the shooting.

Instead of blah-blahing about the clean, healthy rivalry of the football field and the great part played by the Olympic Games in bringing the nations together, it is more useful to inquire how and why this modern cult of sport arose. Most of the games we now play are of ancient origin, but sport does not seem to have been taken very seriously between Roman times and the nineteenth century. Even in the English public schools the games cult did not start till the later part of the last century. Dr Arnold, generally regarded as the founder of the modern public school, looked on games as simply a waste of time. Then, chiefly in England and the United States, games were built up into a heavily-financed activity, capable of attracting vast crowds and rousing savage passions, and the infection spread from country to country. It is the most violently combative sports, football and boxing, that have spread the widest. There cannot be much doubt that the whole thing is bound up with the rise of nationalism – that is, with the lunatic modern habit of identifying oneself with large power units and seeing everything in terms of competitive prestige. Also, organized games are more likely to flourish in urban communities where the average human being lives a sedentary or at least a confined life, and does not get much opportunity for creative labour. In a rustic community a boy or young man works off a good deal of his surplus energy by walking, swimming, snowballing, climbing trees, riding horses, and by various sports involving cruelty to animals, such as fishing, cock-fighting and ferreting for rats. In a big town one must indulge in group activities if one wants an outlet for one's physical strength or for one's sadistic impulses. Games are taken seriously in London and New York, and they were taken seriously in Rome and Byzantium: in the Middle Ages they were played, and probably played with much physical brutality, but they were not mixed up with politics nor a cause of group hatreds.

If you wanted to add to the vast fund of ill-will existing in the world at this moment, you could hardly do it better than by a series of football matches between Jews and Arabs, Germans and Czechs, Indians and British, Russians and Poles, and Italians and Jugoslavs, each match to be watched by a mixed audience of 100,000 spectators. I do not, of course, suggest that sport is one of the main causes of international rivalry; big-scale sport is itself, I think, merely another effect of the causes that have produced nationalism. Still, you do make things worse by sending forth a team of eleven men, labelled as national champions, to do battle against some rival team, and allowing it to be felt on all sides that whichever nation is defeated will 'lose face'.

I hope, therefore, that we shan't follow up the visit of the Dynamos by sending a British team to the U.S.S.R. If we must do so, then let us send a second-rate team which is sure to be beaten and cannot be claimed to represent Britain as a whole. There are quite enough real causes of trouble already, and we need not add to them by encouraging young men to kick each other on the shins amid the roars of infuriated spectators.

Permissions Acknowledgements

Extract from *A Room With a View* is reproduced with permission from The Provost and Scholars of King's College, Cambridge and The Society of Authors as the *E. M. Forster Estate*.

The Good Companions by J. B. Priestley is published by Great Northern Books.

'The Subaltern's Love Song' by John Betjeman from *John Betjeman Collected Poems* (1958) reproduced with permission of Hodder and Stoughton through PLS Clear.